ROSIE NO-NAME

and the Forest of Forgetting

ROSIE NO-NAME

and the Forest of Forgetting

❊❊❊

Gareth Owen

Holiday House / New York

PRINTED IN THE UNITED STATES OF AMERICA

Library of Congress Cataloging-in-Publication Data
Owen, Gareth.
Rosie no-name and the forest of forgetting / Gareth Owen.
p.   cm.
Summary: Eleven-year-old Rosie fights for her life after she falls
through the crumbling stairway in a mysterious old house.
ISBN 0-8234-1266-0 (hardcover : alk. paper)
[1. Witches—Fiction.]   I. Title.
PZ7.097115Ro   1996   96-11217   CIP   AC
[Fic]—dc20

For Alice

ROSIE NO-NAME

and the Forest of Forgetting

SUMMER 1916

When she heard the strange voice calling, Beth stopped. She turned this way and that, peering into the dark trees.

'Row, is that you? Row?'

Branches cracked above her and she gasped with fear. The wings of a startled pigeon whirred above her.

'Row? I know it's you.'

The silence beat upon her. She cupped her hands about her mouth and yelled with all her strength to show she wasn't frightened.

'Row! Stop being silly. You don't frighten me.'

But her confidence ebbed in the dark strangeness of the wood. She heard a voice whispering. What was it saying?

'Beeeth!'

She felt the thump of her heart.

'Beeeth!'

Her name. Hers, echoing from the gnarled oaks that surrounded her.

She turned this way and that.

'Beeeth!'

There it was again.

'Listen to me,' the voice whispered. 'Listen. I am the Witch of the Dark Pool. You'll never see your sister again. Never. I have taken her down.'

'Row, don't!'

'Down into my dark pool that has no end. And now, Beth, it's your turn.'

Beth turned this way and that. Tears of fear started at her eyes.

'You're horrid,' she said. 'Frightening me.'

With a crash of breaking branches a dark shadow dropped behind her. Beth screamed. She covered her face with her hands and, stepping back, fell to the ground. She looked up fearfully.

Her sister was laughing. 'Oh, Beth, you should have seen your face.'

Beth stuck out her lower lip. 'I knew it was you all the time,' she said. She stood up, brushing the dirt from her long skirt. 'Just one of your stupid tricks.'

Row looked at her.

'Then, if you weren't frightened, Beth, why did you scream and cry?'

Beth fisted the tears away. 'Not crying,' she said.

Row smiled. 'Did you really think I was the witch? How silly you are, Beth. You really are the silliest person I know. You don't really believe there's an old witch, do you?'

'Of course not. I knew it . . . '

But Row had turned and was running deeper into the wood. 'Come on. I've got something to show you.'

Beth hung back thinking of her younger brother playing by the river. In the Nursery there would be muffins and cook's best strawberry jam and lemonade. If they were late, although Row was the eldest, it would be she, Beth, who would get the blame. It wasn't fair.

Row pulled a face. 'Oh, don't be such a goody-goody. If you don't come you won't see my secret place.'

Beth hesitated. 'Secret?'

'Shan't tell you now,' said Row.

When Beth caught up with her Row was sitting leaning upon one arm on a steep bank staring down into the dark pool.

'Do be careful,' said Beth. She crouched a safe distance from the slope. 'Is that your secret? Why, it's only a pond.'

Row untied the red ribbon that bound up her long dark hair and let her tresses fall. 'Not an ordinary pond, stupid. A magic pool.'

'Magic?'

Row glanced about her as though she feared someone might be listening. In spite of herself Beth leaned forward to catch her words.

'They say,' she whispered, 'that if you come at midnight when the moon shines clear and let your hair touch the water, when it clears you'll see a face there.'

'Of course,' scoffed Beth, 'your reflection.'

Row sighed. 'You don't understand anything, do you. Not your own face, silly. A stranger's. A special face.'

2

Beth was sure that Row was making it up as she went along but in spite of herself she was curious. 'Whose face?'

Row opened her eyes wide. Her voice was a whisper. 'Why, the man you'll marry, of course.'

'You're making it up. It's one of grandmama's stories.'

'Not a story. I'm coming back tonight to see. Will you come, Beth? Will you?'

Beth shook her head. 'No. What would Mummy say if she found out?'

'What would Mummy say?' mocked Row. 'Anyway, no use your coming. You wouldn't see anything.'

'Why not?'

'Because you'll never marry, that's why. No man would have you.'

'Why, Row, why?'

'Because you're too plain, that's why.'

'Who says?'

'Everybody. Nobody will ever love you. You'll end your days all alone drinking tea and nibbling biscuits in a house full of dust and emptiness.'

Beth clambered to her feet angrily. 'You're horrible to say such things. I hate you.' She stamped her foot. For the second time tears started at her eyes.

Row swung her waist-long hair so that it glanced across the pool. Water showered like diamonds. For an instant a pillar of sunlight pierced the gloom. Row whispered, 'But I shall. Do you know why, Beth? Because I'm beautiful.'

'But . . . ' began Beth but her sister cut her short.

'Look!' she exclaimed, pointing excitedly. 'Look there!'

'Where?'

'There. Can't you see him?'

Beth stared but saw nothing.

'You're making it all up. You'll go to Hell for your lies.' And she turned on her heel and walked away. 'I'm going now. It'll be you who'll get into trouble if you're late. I'm fed up with taking the blame.'

Row looked after her. She felt sorry for what she'd done. She loved Beth but somehow she couldn't help teasing her. It was almost a habit.

3

'Beth, don't go. I didn't mean it. I won't do it again. Promise, Beth.'

But Beth walked on without turning. This time she was going home whatever happened. She was determined not to turn back.

Row watched her. She couldn't help smiling. How ridiculous her sister looked stumbling across the uneven grass trying to look dignified.

'Beth,' she called once more, 'I didn't mean it.'

But she was still smiling, not seeing that the dark water behind her had parted; not seeing the long, curved nails breaking the surface.

'Beth, I'm sorry. Please let's be friends,' she called, not feeling the bony hand that reached silently out for her, folding the shimmering dark hair into a knot about the fist. And when she felt it and tried to pull away, alas, it was too late and she felt herself slipping down that mossy bank. One cry she gave; one last, despairing, forlorn cry.

'Beth. Help me, Beth!'

Before the dark and bottomless waters engulfed her.

And Beth was proud of herself. Things were going to change. She wouldn't be taken in any more. She ran through the wood and, emerging, saw her brother crouched by a small tributary of the river, damming the flow with broken sticks and stones. She told him it was time for tea but he pretended not to hear. He stood up. 'Who was screaming?' he shouted.

'Only Row,' shouted Beth. 'Playing silly games. Playing witches.'

The boy turned from his sister to the forest. 'Witches?' he murmured to himself and smiled.

Beth turned from him and walked towards the boat. 'Are you coming for tea?'

The boy stared after her. He loved Row's stories. There was always something dangerous about them. He crossed his fingers behind his back. 'In a minute,' he shouted.

He watched Beth pull the boat across the river and then climb the grassy bank towards the house; saw her silhouetted against the great windows that flashed back the July sun.

As soon as she had disappeared into the house he smiled to himself and turned towards the dark fringes of the forest. He called his sister's name and listened. But there was no reply. Nor would she ever reply though he might listen till the end of time. For the black waters had closed once more. Closed over her sweet dark head, and things were as they had always been.

1

Just before it all happened Rosie was standing in a country lane watching helplessly as her father drove off the road and into a ditch.

He got out and stared at the back wheels. 'Stupid car!' he muttered.

'I shouted you to stop,' said Rosie.

Mr Oliver kicked a tyre. 'What did you want to go and do that for?' he said to the car.

Rosie thought, that's him all over. Blaming on his car the faults of his driving. But then she had to excuse him. It was the first time he'd driven for four years and if it hadn't been for the baby Rosie's mum wouldn't have let him drive this time.

At five in the morning, Rosie's dad had shaken her awake. 'Emergency, emergency. It's the new lodger. He's arrived early.'

The new lodger was what Dad called the baby.

They'd driven through the dawn to the maternity hospital in town as if they'd robbed a bank and the whole Lancashire police force were on their tail. Rosie's mother sat beside her husband issuing crisp instructions, her hands resting on the shelf of her stomach. 'Brake, darling. No, the left one's the brake. Mind that milk van. No, red is the one you're supposed to stop on.'

It had been an exciting journey.

And after all the rush it had turned out to be a false alarm. But as the doctor thought the baby might arrive any time in the next forty-eight hours he had decided to keep Rosie's mother in.

Gazing over his shoulder in order to reverse out of the hospital car park her father let in the clutch. The car had rolled forward into a neat privet hedge.

'What's that stupid hedge doing in the middle of a car park?' grumbled Mr Oliver.

'You want reverse,' Rosie said.

'What?'

'Reverse. It's got an R on it.'

Her father glanced down. 'So it has.'

They had shot backwards in a long shuddering arc sending showers of shale spinning into the air. A toy poodle which had been enjoying a peaceful morning stroll leapt whimpering into the arms of his owner.

'Anybody behind?' her father called.

'Not now you've killed them all,' said Rosie.

As they drove across the car park to the main road the lady shook her fist and shouted.

''Morning,' replied Rosie's dad giving a cheery wave. 'Do we know that lady?'

'I hope not,' said Rosie.

They filtered into the morning traffic leaving the town through the East Gate and crossing the river. Rosie buried herself in her book in the back seat so she wouldn't see the accident she was sure was about to happen.

The sun shone. Her father began one of his mumbling, tuneless hums. 'What you reading, Rosie?'

'Book,' said Rosie.

'That's novel,' said her father. 'I mean what's it called?'

Rosie dragged her eyes from the page. The inside wheels were almost on the verge.

'Watch out or we'll be in the ditch,' she said.

'Funny title,' said her father.

Rosie groaned. 'It's called *The Witch of the Dark Pool*,' said Rosie.

She returned to the story, trying to find the place. But Mr Oliver was feeling chatty.

'Sounds interesting,' he said. 'Who wrote it?'

'Guess,' said Rosie.

'Give up,' said her father without pausing.

'You did,' said Rosie.

'Did I really?' said Rosie's father. 'Must have been a few years ago.'

'Ages,' said Rosie. 'At least six years ago.'

Rosie searched for her place once more. She had just managed to find it when her father said, 'What happens?'

'Well,' said Rosie, 'there's this old witch who hates children because they're young and she's old and ugly and jealous and

7

everything so she pulls them into this dark pool that has no end and keeps them in a dungeon until they die.'

'Sounds reasonable,' said Mr Oliver.

'Better than the boring old books you write now about the lives of boring old people,' said Rosie.

'True,' said her father, turning off the main road and into a country lane, 'but it pays for the cornflakes.'

Rosie looked about her. 'Aren't we going home?'

Her father was peering from left to right. 'Oh, didn't I tell you? I've got to interview this general chap this morning. New biography. Won't be too long. You'll like the house. It's very old. Might even be haunted. Damn!'

He trod on the brakes suddenly and the car screeched to a halt. Two black and white cows contemplated them steadily over a low hedge, wondering no doubt why the morning suddenly smelt of rubber.

'Missed it,' said her dad looking back over his shoulder.

'Missed what?' said Rosie rubbing her nose which she had banged against the front seat.

Her dad pointed back up the road to a concealed drive. 'That's where the general lives. Stupid car went past it.'

The road was deserted. Her dad said, 'Nothing for it but to turn round.'

Rosie climbed out and stood to one side ready to shout 'Whoa!'

'Watch out you don't drive into the ditch,' she shouted as he revved up the engine.

'No chance of that,' said her father jovially.

And that's how they came to be standing in a deserted lane at eleven o'clock one Monday morning looking at a green Rover as it lay tilted, nose in the air, with the rear tyres embedded securely in a muddy ditch.

They tried pushing it. Then they put stones and mats and branches under the back wheels but the car merely spun its back wheels in the mud and sank lower.

Rosie suggested ringing the AA but there was no phone in sight. Her father looked up at the sky as though the answer might lie up there somewhere. Across the brow of a hill a tractor chugged. Clouds of seagulls flocked in its wake.

'I'm going to ask that farmer if he'll give me a heave-ho out of this,' said her father. 'Look, you'd better stop here and warn any cars.'

While her father tramped up the ploughed hill Rosie leaned on the bonnet. There wasn't a car in sight. The cows had given up thinking about rubber and had gone back to their first love, grass.

Rosie thought, Things always happen in threes. First there was the baby that didn't arrive. Now we've ended up in a ditch. I wonder what the third thing will be. To fill in the time she decided to write the events of the day into her diary. She sat in the front seat of the car and unlocked her Life Diary. On the first page was written in Rosie's best six-year-old printing

ROSIE JANE OLIVER.
HER LIFE.

Underneath she had written her address:

MY BEDROOM
TURN RIGHT AT THE TOP OF THE STAIRS
NEXT TO THE BATHROOM
35 HUNTSVIEW ROAD
WEST FELSGARTH
LANCASHIRE
ENGLAND
GREAT BRITAIN
EUROPE
THE WESTERN HEMISPHERE
THE WORLD
THE UNIVERSE
SOMEWHERE IN SPACE
NOW.

All Rosie's life was in this book. She read the first entry she had made five years ago.

Got up. My name is Rosie. Go to bed.

Exciting day that must have been, thought Rosie.

She turned to the day's date, unscrewed her biro and began to write:

Up early. Mummy having baby. False alarm. Doctor said it will come tomorrow or the next day. Daddy nearly ran over a poodle. Then into a ditch. We are going to see a General something-or-other. Dad is writing his life. Dad has gone to get the farmer who . . .

She heard voices and looking up saw her father and the farmer staring at the back wheels. Rosie locked her diary and shoved it into the pocket of her jeans. The farmer pushed his greasy cap back and scratched his chin. Rosie could hear his black nails rasping on his beard.

'Looks like you're in a ditch all right,' he said.

Brilliant, thought Rosie. I could have told you that for nothing and kept the change. But she didn't say anything.

'I'll get a chain and some tackle,' said the farmer.

'I'll come with you,' said her dad.

He turned to Rosie and smiled. Rosie knew that smile. It said, *Look, I'm your father and I can tell you to do something if I want to but I'd rather ask you and then you can offer.*

He cleared his throat. Here it comes, thought Rosie.

'Rosie, be a good girl. Run up to the house and tell the general I'm going to be late.'

Mmm, thought Rosie, 'good girl' means doing what they want you to do. Mmm.

She looked about her as if she was waiting for something.

'It's worth 50p extra pocket money,' said her father.

That's what she had been waiting for. 'Pound,' she said.

'60p.'

'Seventy-five,' said Rosie.

'Done,' said her father.

Rosie smiled. 'I'd have done it for nothing,' she said.

'Oh, that's good,' said her father starting to put the money back in his pocket.

'But a bargain is a bargain.'

'I love you, Rosie,' said her dad and kissed the top of her head.

'Why?' asked Rosie.

'What d'you mean why? What sort of question is that?'

'Well, is it because I'm doing what you want me to do? Or because I'm young or because I'm your daughter?'

'All of that,' said her dad. 'And you're smart. Is that OK?'

'It'll do,' said Rosie, 'but keep reminding me.'

She hugged her dad and walked back up the lane towards the entrance.

'I'd love you even if you weren't smart,' shouted her dad.

'What's that?' said the farmer.

At the double white gates that led into the tree-shaded lane Rosie turned. She wanted to make a picture of her father in her head. She always did this. It was like a mind photograph that she could carry about with her in case . . . Well, she didn't know what it was in case of. It was just something she always did. She waved a big wave. But her dad had his head down and was talking to the farmer. What if he doesn't turn round and I never see him again, she thought and a shiver passed over her whole being. So she shouted and shouted until he turned and lifted both his arms in the air as though he was signalling to a jumbo jet where to land. Rosie was content. Now she had her photo.

She closed the gate and ran up the narrow gravel path between the tall trees towards the large house. She entered the stone porch and just before she pulled the bell wondered again what the third thing would be. She shook the feeling away, pulling down hard on the bell.

11

2

The door bell didn't seem to be working so Rosie banged with her fist on the large studded door. To her surprise it creaked open a few inches. She pushed her head round.

'Hello, anyone home?'

There was no answer.

Feeling rather like a burglar she slipped inside to find herself in a large, oak-panelled hallway. A grandfather clock ticked solemnly in the corner. From the high walls family portraits gazed down upon her as if to say, 'What do you think you're doing in our house?'

On a large oak table stood a number of framed photographs of men in top hats and black coats sitting on horses and ladies in long skirts smiling rather haughtily out at the world. One photograph particularly caught her eye. It was of a young boy in a dog cart. He stared out as if about to give Rosie an order.

Looking closer she felt something tickling the back of her neck, as though ten spiders were crawling up it and into her hair. She put up her hand. But there were no spiders. It was the hair on her nape standing on end. She had the strangest and most certain feeling that someone's eyes were on her. Nervously she turned round.

But the hall was deserted.

Strange, thought Rosie, looking about her.

Then she saw. High on the opposite wall a pair of beautiful dark eyes stared directly into hers. From a painting.

You berk, Rosie, fancy being spooked by a silly old painting, she thought to herself. She moved closer. The eyes belonged to a girl of about her own age. Around her throat she wore a long white scarf and about her lips a mocking smile played mischievously. Like a cat, thought Rosie. It was a strange face. Beautiful, in a way that managed to be happy and immensely sad at the same time. Rosie looked about her. She wanted a closer look at this beautiful girl. She picked up a chair and stood on it. The eyes seemed to look straight into hers as though the girl in the painting knew all her secrets.

She was leaning forward to wipe the dust from the glass when she heard a woman's voice from inside the house. She hadn't done anything wrong but she felt guilty being in the house without being invited, especially as she was standing on a chair. She jumped down hurriedly, brushed the dirt off the chair and replaced it next to the door that led into the house. She intended to tiptoe across the hall and out of the front door but just at that moment the door behind which she was standing swung open and a lady walked through. Rosie flattened herself against the wall behind the door. The lady was so close that Rosie could have stretched out her hand and touched her back. She was dressed in the same tightly buttoned, high-collared blouse and long skirt as the ladies Rosie had seen in the photographs.

Rosie wanted to say something. But it was difficult to know what. It was complicated trying to think of an innocent reason for hiding behind a door in somebody's house. And the longer her silence lasted the more guilty Rosie felt.

The lady raised her arms. 'Are you listening?' she demanded with a tone of such authority that Rosie almost said 'yes' aloud.

'It was here, across this very floor that she walked. Can you feel it? Feel her presence? Through this very hall she ran, laughing gaily. Utterly unaware that she was making her last journey.' Her voice sank to a whisper. 'Her very last journey to that far off country from whose bourn no traveller returns.'

Rosie realized that she must be addressing a crowd of people standing on the other side of the door out of her line of sight. 'Excuse me . . . ' she began softly. But the lady swept through the outside door not hearing her.

'Now to the West Wing and the scene of the great fire. Follow me.'

Rosie waited to let the crowd through. But nobody came. She peeped through the inner door. There was no one. Where was everybody? She ran across the hall out through the main door and into the courtyard. She was just in time to see the lady disappearing round the corner of the house still talking and gesticulating. Rosie frowned. How strange, she thought. A sudden roaring woke her from her thoughts. It was accompanied by a

13

strange wailing like someone moaning in extreme pain. She peeped through the lounge door once more.

A white-haired man with a bristling moustache was walking slowly back and forth hoovering the carpet and singing loudly and tunelessly to himself.

Rosie crossed to him.

'Excuse me.'

The sound of the Hoover drowned her voice. She tapped the old gentleman on the shoulder. He gave a little start of surprise.

'Sorry to frighten you,' said Rosie. 'I did knock but nobody answered. The door was open so I came in.'

The old gentleman cupped his hand to his ear. 'What's that?'

Rosie shouted. 'I DID KNOCK . . . ' she began.

The old man switched off the Hoover.

' . . . BUT NOBODY HEARD.'

Rosie's voice rang round the lounge. Somewhere deep in the house a dog began to bark. She lowered her voice. 'I came in, I hope you don't mind.'

He looked at her over his spectacles. 'Are you public?'

Rosie shook her head.

'Ah, I know, you must be the help. Elizabeth said you'd be coming. Look, you'd better carry on.' He handed her the Hoover. 'Elizabeth will explain what needs doing when she comes back from whatever she's doing.'

'I was told to find the general . . . ' Rosie began.

'Yes, that's me,' said the man. 'Now, you'd better get a move on, there's lots to do.'

A phone began to ring.

'But I'm not the help,' began Rosie but her words were drowned as the old man switched on the Hoover.

'I'M NOT THE HELP!' she repeated.

'That's right, you carry on,' said the man. 'I've got to answer the phone.'

He hurried away through the door into a study leaving Rosie holding the roaring vacuum cleaner. She switched off the machine and hurried after him. He was talking into a phone.

'Excuse me,' said Rosie.

The general looked up at her in some surprise. 'Finished already? That was quick. Why not make a start in here.' He spoke

14

into the phone. 'No, just talking to the help. Yes . . . yes. Goodbye.'

He began to walk out of the room humming.

Rosie ran after him. 'I'm not the help,' she said.

'Not?'

'No.'

'And you're not public?'

The way he said it made Rosie feel like a lavatory or a library.

'Certainly not,' said Rosie with some fire.

'Oh!' said the general. 'Then who are you?'

'Rosie,' said Rosie with a touch of defiance.

'Rosie?'

'Yes, and I've come with a message from my father.'

'Your father? What's he done?'

'He's in a ditch.'

'A ditch! Goodness.' The general was looking about him with a worried expression on his face. 'Is he a . . . er . . . tramp?'

Rosie laughed. 'Of course not. It was an accident.'

'Accident. Oh, I see. Poor chap. I suppose you want some help to get him out.'

'Oh no, the farmer's doing that.'

'Farmer?'

'With a tractor and some chains.'

'Tractor? Chains?' The general stared at her. 'Your father, is he . . . er . . . ' he held both arms out in front of him, 'is he a large sort of chap?'

'We were in a car,' Rosie explained.

'Aaaah.' The general gave a sigh of relief. 'A car. Of course, yes.'

'We were looking for your house. Daddy drove past the drive and when he turned round he sort of went into the ditch.'

Dawn rose in the general's eyes. 'Penny dropped,' he said. 'Ah, then you must be the writer . . . er . . . chappy's daughter, Mr . . . er . . . Mr . . . '

'Oliver,' said Rosie.

'Of course, and he sent you to tell me he was going to be late.' Rosie nodded.

'Good. Good. And your name is?'

'Rosie.'

15

'Rosie. Of course, you said. Yes.'

He smiled and gave a little cough. There was a silence. The general looked around as though he hoped someone might come in who could speak to her.

He's not used to talking to children, Rosie thought.

The general coughed. 'Tell me, er . . . '

'Rosie.'

'Rosie. Would you like a drink while we're waiting?'

Rosie nodded. 'Yes, please.'

'Good. Capital. How about a gin and tonic?'

Rosie pulled a face. 'Ugh, no thank you. I'm only eleven.'

'Of course. I've got the very thing.'

He went to a cabinet in the corner of the room and returned with a glass of orange for her and a whisky for himself. They sat in the window seat which looked down through a shrubbery and a sloping stretch of grassland to a river. There was a silence. She sensed that the general was desperately trying to think of something to ask her.

'So,' the general said. 'Well, there we are then. Yes.'

Rosie smiled back and sipped at the orange. A small kitten leapt up on to the window seat. 'Well, your father's a writer, eh? That must be exciting. To read books and think that your father wrote them.'

Rosie shook her head. 'Don't read them any more.'

'You don't? Good Lord, why's that?'

'Well, I used to. And I still read the old ones that he wrote when I was little but he's not a very good writer any more.'

'Have you told him that?'

'Sort of. Well, you see, it's not exactly the books. It's what he writes about. When I was little he wrote really good adventure stories. He'd tell them to me at night when I was in bed, making them up as he went along, and then later he'd write them down and make them into books.'

'Into books and you'd been there when he made them up. That must have been fun.' He smiled and nodded. 'These . . . er . . . adventure stories, what were they about?'

'Well, me mainly,' said Rosie.

'You!'

'Well, sort of. But the things that happened were exaggerated.

16

They were all called things like: *Rosie and the Caterpillar, Rosie in the Magic Mountain,* or *Rosie's Voyage under the Sea* and so on. And I just had these incredible adventures.'

The general sipped his whisky. 'But tell me, Rosie, why don't you read them any more?'

'Because he doesn't write those kind of stories any more. Now he writes these boring biographies about boring old people . . . '

'Like me, you mean.'

'Yes,' said Rosie without thinking. She put her hand to her mouth. 'Oh no. Oh, I mean . . . '

She was blushing down to her waist.

'I'm sorry . . . I . . . '

The general waved his hand. 'No, no. You're perfectly right. I am boring. D'you know,' he lowered his voice as though telling a secret and Rosie leaned forward, 'because I knew your father was coming to ask me questions about my life, I started looking back over my diaries. And oh, my goodness, you've never read such a load of boring old tosh in your born days. Now, if only I'd kept a diary when I was young, how exciting that would have been. Each day was a lifetime. Something was always happening. Swimming in the river, climbing trees and falling out, breaking legs, fighting, running away. Do you know,' he looked about him as though fearful someone might overhear, 'once I even died.'

Rosie looked at him. Was he making fun of her?

'Died!'

'Oh yes.' The general chuckled. 'Burnt to death.'

'Burnt to death,' gasped Rosie, her mouth open with amazement. 'How awful!'

'Yes. Mother was pretty upset I can tell you.'

'But . . . ' Rosie wasn't quite sure how to put it. 'But you're still here.'

'What?' The general looked down at himself. 'So I am. You're absolutely right, Rosie.' He lowered his voice once more. 'Shall I tell you a secret?' He plucked up the kitten and began to scratch it behind the ears. The kitten purred and butted him with its head. 'Hello, Thomas. Say hello to Rosie.'

The kitten yawned hugely.

'What was I saying?'

17

'You were telling me about dying,' said Rosie who couldn't wait to hear the rest of the story.

'Ah yes. Well, of course I didn't really die or else I wouldn't be here talking to you, would I? But everybody thought I had, you see. When I was ten or eleven I was for ever running away. Very worrying for everybody. Especially my mother.'

'Where did you go to?'

'Nowhere in particular. Just there and back to see what it was like. My mother thought I was looking for somebody. Perhaps she was right. And there was . . . Well, I don't want to go into all that. Anyway, this one particular time I stayed out all night with this strange girl.'

'Strange?' said Rosie. 'What was strange about her?'

'Well, she didn't really exist, you see.'

'Didn't exist?'

'No, not really.' He sipped his whisky. 'Rosie, I don't know if you ever had an invisible friend?'

Rosie nodded. 'When I was four.'

'Well, I had one too.'

'When you were eleven?'

'Yes, I know,' said the general, 'should have grown out of it by then, I suppose. But there you are. Perhaps I was lonely, I don't know. Anyway, there we were, me and . . . '

'Your invisible friend.'

'That's right, and we stayed out all night.'

'All night?'

'Yes. But by coincidence that was the very night the fire started in the West Wing where the nursery was. And the whole lot went up like a tinder box. Woosh! Just like that.'

'How awful. Was anybody killed?'

'Apart from me, you mean? No. Everybody gathered on the lawn at about four in the morning and was counted. And then, of course, they discovered that I was missing. Oh dear, what a to-do there was then. Of course, everybody presumed I'd died in the fire.'

'But you hadn't.'

'Of course not. I was out in the woods. It was very naughty of me really. My mother went distracted. She'd have plunged back into the flames if they hadn't stopped her. I was only young so I

18

didn't think of all the trouble I was causing. Just an adventure for me. So when I walked back up to the house I was surprised to see everybody walking about and all the lights on. Mother got quite a fright when she saw me. Well, she thought I was dead, you see. And there I was large as life. Then she cried and hugged me so tight I thought I would crack. Then she shouted at me then hugged me again. Then shouted at me again. Then cried again.'

'My mum did that when I got lost in the museum that time,' said Rosie.

The general nodded. 'Mothers do,' he said. He smiled at her for a moment. 'D'you know, Rosie, I'm enjoying this conversation.' He stood up suddenly. 'Tell you what, would you like to see where the fire was?'

'Can I?' said Rosie.

'Of course. Come along.' He paused and leaned across and opened the large window. 'Just a moment. Tell my sister where we're going.'

He flung open the window. 'Just going to show Rosie the West Wing,' he shouted down the lawn.

Rosie saw the tall figure of the lady she'd seen earlier.

She heard her voice winging back. 'Rosie? Who on earth's Rosie?'

'Writer chap's daughter. Here she is.' He whispered, 'Wave, Rosie. That'll make her happy.'

Rosie waved.

'Have you finished the hoovering?'

He glanced at Rosie with eyebrows raised. 'Did we?'

Rosie shook her head.

The general winked at Rosie. 'All done,' he called.

The general's sister was shouting something else but he pretended not to hear and closed the window. 'Come along,' he said.

They walked down a corridor together. 'Come along, Thomas.'

The kitten trotted behind them, tail in the air.

Rosie was thinking about the general's sister. Why was she walking about talking to crowds of people who weren't there? Was she bonkers? It was a difficult point to raise. She cleared her throat. 'Why does your sister wear old-fashioned clothes?'

'Ah, special day, you see.'

'Special?'

19

'Yes. First time we're opening the place to the public. She'll be the guide. So she's having a rehearsal.'

'Oh, I see,' said Rosie. 'I thought . . . '

'You thought she was bonkers?'

Rosie laughed. 'No, I thought she was a ghost.'

'A ghost!' The general gave a laugh. 'A ghost. Oh, she'll enjoy that. Wait till I tell her.'

They had stopped in a stone-flagged hallway. Through a large window at the end Rosie could see the drive down which she had walked earlier.

'This is it,' said the general spreading his arms and turning round slowly. 'Scene of the famous fire.'

Rosie looked round. To her left a dark wooden stairway curved upwards. Where it joined the landing several stairs and a section of the upper flooring were missing. The underneath was blackened and the walls still charred. Across the bottom step was a wooden barrier with a notice pinned to it warning people not to climb the stairs.

'Never got it fixed,' explained the general. 'Well, it's tucked away. We don't really use it. Apart from that, there wasn't the money in the bank, you see. Partly why we're opening the place to the public. Pay for the repairs. But for the moment it's exactly as it was when I came running back and they all thought I was a spirit from the dead.' He laughed at the memory. Rosie had a feeling that he'd rather enjoyed being dead and frightening everybody. 'What I should have done was to reappear at my own funeral. Like Tom Sawyer. Pop up from behind my own coffin and wave. "Hello, everybody, I'm back".' He laughed again, the laugh turning into a long bout of coughing. He blew his nose and indicated the walls. 'What d'you think of the pictures, eh?'

There were five of them. Rosie recognized one immediately. It was of the girl she'd been looking at in the hall when the general's sister had walked through.

Just then she heard the sound of a car; gears crunched noisily.

'That'll be my dad,' said Rosie.

'Ah,' said the general. 'Out of the ditch and back in the land of the living. You stay here, Rosie. I'll bring him round. You have an explore. But whatever you do, don't go up the staircase, will you. It's very unsteady. Promise!'

20

She gave her word and the old man was about to set off when he turned back to her. 'Here's a little quiz for you. Have a look at those pictures. Tell me if there's someone you recognize. I'll ask you when I get back.'

And he set off at a surprisingly brisk pace for such an old man; head upright, shoulders back, stepping out as though to a drum only he could hear. She heard his shoes ringing rhythmically long after she had lost sight of him.

She walked over to the painting and looked up at it. The girl was dressed in a long white dress. She stood on a cliff top gazing out over the sea. The sky was azure and cloudless. There was not a boat to be seen. Nothing. Yet the girl gazed with a concentrated expression as though on something that no one else could see. About her throat was tied the same long, lace scarf.

She looked at the other paintings and was about to follow the general to see how her father had got on when she heard the sound of faint scratching. She looked up to see the tiny kitten's face staring through the carved and blackened supports. Its mouth opened wide and it released a pitiful and quavering cry. It stretched out a tentative front paw as far as it dared. But the gap was too great.

'Oh, pussy,' said Rosie. 'You naughty thing. How did you get up there?'

Somehow it had managed to crawl across the gap and on to the further side of the broken stairway and now it couldn't get back. The miaows became louder and more plaintive. They rent the air. The kitten had drawn back and was gazing at the drop beneath it. Then it leaned forward as if about to jump.

'Don't jump,' Rosie implored. 'I'll get somebody.'

She looked about her but the long corridor was deserted. And supposing she went for help, by that time the kitten might have grown desperate and jumped. The stair nearest to the wall was still precariously intact. She knew she had given her word, but this was an emergency.

She dropped to her knees and hugging the stone wall crawled up the stairway a slow step at a time. In certain parts the treads had completely broken away and she had to step across. Through the blackened boards she could see the stone floor of the hallway far below her.

21

'Don't look down, Rosie,' she instructed herself.

But she couldn't help it and a dizziness seized her. She paused, collected herself, then began to crawl onwards and upwards one slow inch at a time. At last she had only to reach out and she would be able to grasp the kitten.

'Come on, Thomas.'

But as she spoke the kitten drew back.

She stretched further. 'Stupid cat, I'm only trying to help you.'

And then she was touching the thick fur on the side of the kitten's body. Just a few more inches. She stretched again. But just as her hand was about to reach and close round its tiny body the kitten turned and scampered away.

'Oh spit!' Rosie shouted. 'You stupid cat.' She would have to get help after all.

She turned slowly. But as she withdrew her right knee from the stair the floor opened up beneath her. Her falling seemed to last for a long time. Somehow she felt no fear. She had time to think to herself, Oh, I'm falling. She felt somehow that she was watching herself and yet at the same time falling.

She could see the pieces of wood dropping about her and hear the sound of the stone crumbling and crashing to the floor. She was even able to take in the painting on the wall; the young girl in a long white summer dress staring out on a sky and sea so pure that it was like the first morning of the world. So clear was the picture that she thought she heard the deep roar of the ocean and the far gulls crying.

And then she was on the ground and was surprised to discover that she wasn't in any pain. She felt herself all over to make sure and then slowly stood up flexing and bending her arms and legs to make sure that everything was working. The kitten sat beneath the picture watching her solemnly.

At least you're safe, thought Rosie. Look at all the trouble you caused.

And the kitten stared back at her, its head cocked to one side, and then began to wash its face with bent paw as if this sort of thing happened every day.

From the corridor to her right she heard the sound of running feet and her father appeared, his face white with anxiety. Rosie waved.

'It's all right, Dad, I'm fine,' she called. 'Look, I'm not hurt at all.'

But the people gathered about something on the floor and didn't seem to see her. Her father was stooping now on one knee and weeping. He held something in his arms. Somebody brought a blanket and another ran off to telephone. Rosie couldn't understand why her father was so upset.

'Daddy,' she cried. 'It's me, Rosie. I'm over here.'

And then just as she despaired of getting anyone to take any notice of her, a figure came walking down the stairs towards her. A girl in a long white dress, the long scarf rising and falling as it trailed behind her. She smiled at Rosie as she passed and beckoned her towards the open window where the long net curtain billowed. Rosie looked from her father and then back at the girl. Once more she tried to get his attention but he was too busy talking to somebody else.

Oh well, thought Rosie, if you won't take any notice of me I'm going out to play.

The girl was still smiling. Her long hair lifted in the breeze as she stepped out of the window on to the long sloping lawn that led down to the river. She gave a last smiling glance at Rosie and beckoned her to follow. For a moment Rosie hesitated but nobody seemed to be taking any notice of her so she ran to the open window, leaping lightly on to the low sill. She stood for a moment feeling the cool wind on her face. The girl was running down the long slope of green grass towards the river. On the far bank, in the shadow of some trees, a black horse stood motionless as a statue and behind him a black carriage. An elbow rested on the small window. The fingers tapped impatiently.

As Rosie hesitated the girl stopped and looked back, smiling. Then she raised her right hand high in the air. She was clutching something small and red. At first Rosie couldn't make out what it was. Then she knew. 'My diary,' she whispered. 'She's stolen my diary.'

The girl smiled at her for a moment then she stepped into a flat-bottomed boat and drifted out and across the river. For the whole journey she stood staring back. Her long white dress and long hair lifted and swung in the breeze. And then she was on the far bank and running towards the trees. She stood out white and clear against the dark trunks. Once more she beckoned. Rosie gave one last look to her father before leaping down on to the sweet green grass. And then she too was running.

3

'Hey, wait for me,' Rosie cried racing down the slope. She was surprised how fast she was running. She had the feeling that anything was possible. That she could let her feet leave the ground and fly if she wished. The thought of her flying and circling in the air made her giggle and the giggle very swiftly became a laugh so she decided not to try. Probably very hard to fly and laugh at the same time, she thought. That made her laugh even more so that she almost stumbled and fell. But somehow she managed to keep running in spite of everything.

When she reached the bank the boat was back nestling on her side of the bank. Rosie wondered how the girl had sent it back. Then she noticed that it wasn't an ordinary rowing boat. In fact there were no oars at all. A rope stretched, sagging slightly, across the river attached to a post at either end. Then it doubled back and was wound round a windlass that was bolted to the bottom of the boat.

Ah ha, thought Rosie, she's sent the boat back so that I can chase her. It was a game and the prize was her diary.

She leapt down into the boat and gripped the iron handle of the windlass. Using both hands she began to turn it. It took all her strength at first but by the fourth turn it had become much easier. Slowly the boat nosed out into the stream. Rosie looked back. Now she was half-way across. She could no longer see the house which was hidden behind the slope of the lawn.

There was a soft bump and the prow of the boat ground through soft gravel and stopped.

The 'rowing' had taken more out of her than she thought. Rosie stood bent over for a few moments to get her breath back. She stood up straight and looked about her. A dusty sheeptrack led both ways along the bank of the river. Just to her left it turned and led into the forest. Rosie put her hand to her forehead and scanned the trees. There was no sign of the girl in white.

She ran up the narrow track to the fringe of the wood. Or was it a forest? She wasn't sure what the difference was. Forests sounded darker and more dangerous. Better make sure where she was before she went any further, she thought. She glanced back. She could still see the boat that she had tethered to the weathered post. No chance of her getting lost, she thought. Won't go far. Just a little way in. Don't want to be late or they'll get worried.

It struck her that she wasn't quite sure who 'they' were but it didn't seem strange. She ran about a hundred yards into the forest. There was a huge grey boulder half covered in moss. She scrambled up it and balancing herself at the top gazed about her. The girl was probably hiding behind the trees. Or maybe she had crept up behind her. She turned quickly in order to catch her out. A red squirrel nibbled an acorn that he held between his front paws turning it expertly. He froze and then scurried away in a series of long leaps and up a tree. A crow croaked overhead. Rosie cupped her hands about her mouth and shouted, 'Ready or not, here I come.'

Nothing moved.

She thought she heard a lilting voice singing softly to her right but then it might have been a bird singing. She rubbed her nose. Was that a voice calling her? She turned but she could no longer see the river, let alone the house. Better go back, she thought. But as she turned a patch of white caught her eye. She slid down the boulder and folded her fists into binoculars. There it was again. No doubt about it. The edge of a white scarf. She smiled. Got you, she thought. You've got to be smart to hide from Rosie. Who was it had called her smart? Somebody had. Somewhere. But she couldn't picture the person or the place. Doesn't matter anyway, she thought, the important thing is—it's true. She began to run in a long crouching arc so as to come on the girl from the rear; where she was least expecting it. What a surprise she's going to get, she thought. She planned to give her a fright. Leap out on her with a shout. Well, serves her right pinching my diary. She began to sing under her breath:

'Ha ha ha
Hee hee hee
I can see you
But you can't see me.'

26

She repeated it over and over. She crept silently the last few paces to the tree then leapt out suddenly shouting:

'Can't see MEEEEE!'

She was half laughing. But her laughter stopped when she found herself clutching a scarf that had been left hanging in the branches.

Very smart, thought Rosie. Very, very smart. Nine out of ten, V.G. Gold Star!

She inspected the scarf. In one corner a large A had been printed in ink and underneath it a number: 15312. Perhaps a phone number, Rosie mused. She tied the scarf about her throat and wondered what to do next. She was getting bored with this rather one-sided game that was all Seek and no Find.

She shouted into the forest, 'Look, whoever you are. I know you're there. Very clever to leave the scarf as a decoy.'

She stopped and listened to the silence. 'Look, the game's over now. I have to go back. So can I have my diary, please?'

Again silence.

Rosie spun round scanning the forest. Nothing moved. She shouted angrily at the top of her voice, 'Give me my diary back.'

'Back . . . back . . . back,' rang the echo of her voice.

She thought she saw a movement behind a copse of low bushes but when she got there it was just a leaf moving in the breeze.

She shouted again. 'I'm going to have to take your scarf. I will, you know, unless you let me have my diary back.'

She gritted her teeth and began to breathe swiftly. Don't cry, Rosie, she said aloud. Don't be so pathetic.

She shouted once more to her unseen prey. 'If you think you can make me cry you're wrong, you know.'

She felt a tear run down her nose and on to her lips. She could taste the salt of it.

'Please! Please let me have it back. Please!'

The silence was like a sort of sarcasm. Her tears gave way to extreme anger. 'I hate you,' she screamed. 'Whoever you are, I hate you. I hate you, I hate you, I hate you.' There was a long pause. 'I hate you,' she said once more so there should be no doubt about it.

She began to run heedlessly back and forth shouting continuously. When she could run no more she leaned against a tree trunk panting. There was a stitch in her side. She was taking great gulps of breath. Silence descended like a great darkness out of the branches of the tall trees. For the first time Rosie began to feel nervous. She decided to go home, diary or no diary. Anyway that would teach her. Give her one last chance, she thought. She lifted up her voice again. 'I'm going home now.'

She paused, listening. Counted to three and said, 'I am. I don't care. I'm going. I'm going to count to three and then I'm really going. Honestly.'

And she counted loud and slowly.

But no figure in white emerged from among the great trees.

She turned back the way she thought she had come, grumbling to herself—See if I care. Your loss not mine. Never play with you again, so there—But in her heart her loss was the greatest. What was a measly scarf to the story of her diary; her life story. It was irreplaceable. Nothing could compensate for that. Nothing.

She began to count her steps. She had walked a couple of hundred paces but still there was no sign of the river. She looked about her. Surely she wasn't lost. She strained her eyes through the trees searching for a glimpse of water. To her relief she saw a large grey rock she thought she recognized. She ran towards it. Now she knew where she was. The river would be just beyond it. Keep calm, Rosie, she thought. She ran towards it but no welcoming gleam of water met her eye. Just trees and yet more trees.

For the first time a dreadful panic seized her. Her stomach seemed to rise into her heart and throat. She tried to swallow it down but her throat was swollen and dry. What if she never found her way out of this dark wood? But she had to. She had to. This sort of thing only happened to other people. You read about them in the paper or in books. But not to her. Not to Rosie.

She turned twice in a swift circle looking for a tree or stone that she might recognize. Then on an impulse she began to run blindly hither and thither calling out for her father. She knew it was the wrong thing to do but somehow she couldn't help herself. She ran in this way until she could run no further. Then she sank exhausted onto the pine-needled floor. She gasped oxygen into her lungs. She felt faint with running and panic.

In her mind she attempted to retrace the journey she had taken. Like going backwards down a Monopoly board. But she found she could only get so far. She remembered the girl and the carriage. The scarf and the river and . . . Then there was a great blank. As though everything before that was separated from her by a fog of unknowing. At a certain point her memory stopped. There were vague sensations of how it might have been. Like a dream that you couldn't remember when you woke up no matter how hard you tried. She began to try and picture the street in which she lived. Her house, her mother and father. But there was nothing. Nobody. She ran her fingers through her hair. Who are you, Rosie? Who are you? With relief she said her name: Rosie, Rosie, Rosie . . . But no other name came to her mind. She dropped her head into her hands and great sobs shook her. Through the sobs she moaned, I'm nobody. Nobody.

At last she could cry no more. She slumped down, her back to the tree, staring dully into space. As she did so something caught her eye and slowly the lens of her eye brought it into focus. On the dark bark of an oak opposite her was carved a message of some sort. She clambered to her feet and walked across to the tree. It wasn't a message but someone's name carved neatly with a knife. She read it carefully, whispering the word aloud:

AURORA

and underneath was the date:

1916.

A sudden shaft of sadness pierced her. The girl would be old now. Or perhaps even dead. Then, though she tried to beat it away, an awful thought entered her head. What if *she* never found her way out of the forest either? And later someone came and they found *her* and carved *her* name. Then a worse thought came. What if nobody came. Nobody. And she was left there unknown and unrecorded as though she had never been.

Well, that's not going to happen, she said determinedly. I'm me. I'm Rosie. Then she shouted out loud in the loneliness of the forest. 'I'M ROSIE.' The echo died.

From her pocket she took out a small nail file and began to carve. It took her some time because she wanted to do it well and carefully. She brushed away the chippings. Her name—ROSIE— stood out white and clear against the dark bark. She was pleased with it. Then underneath she printed just as carefully

WAS HERE.

29

She read it over.

ROSIE WAS HERE.

She wanted to carve the date but that was another thing she couldn't remember. Not even the year.

She looked from one carving to the other. It was just as good. Then she glanced back once more. There was something strange about those two names carved side by side. What was it? She glanced again from one to the other. The printing was similar but then she had done that on purpose. Then the truth struck her and she gasped aloud. Where she had carved her name the inner wood was white and new. That was it. The other's name which should have been dark with age stood out as clean and white as the one she had carved but minutes before.

She was struggling with the meaning of this when she thought she heard something moving, rustling in the undergrowth behind her. She froze. And then she slowly turned. There was something there. Or someone; moving amongst the canopy of leaves. She could make out a long brown face and a huge eye. She gulped and whispered, 'Hello, is there someone there?'

The eye stared back unblinking. Slowly, holding her breath, she moved forward, parting the leaves. She breathed a long sigh of relief. A pony stared at her. He snorted and shook his mane. Behind him was a small open two-wheeled carriage. She stroked the pony's long brown nose. 'Hello,' she said, 'who are you? You're a nice old thing, aren't you? Where's your owner?'

Perhaps there was a clue in the carriage. Continuing to speak softly to the pony, stroking him gently, she crept past him and up into the carriage. There was a tartan blanket, on top of which was a brown haversack. She opened it. Inside was a hard-backed notebook, a strange looking bulbous bottle containing what looked like plain water, and a damp napkin. She picked up the book and was about to open it when a voice said, 'Raise your hands in the air and don't move.'

30

4

Nervously Rosie turned her head. At first she could see nothing. Then a shrub swayed slightly in the breeze. Except there was no breeze. The bush moved towards her. Rosie stepped back in alarm, dropping her hands.

'Pardon me,' said the bush in a cultured voice, 'did I give you permission to put your hands down?'

'No,' said Rosie. It was the first time she'd been given orders by a bush, especially one with such a posh voice.

'Then be so good as to remain motionless until I give orders to the contrary,' said the bush.

'Pardon?' said Rosie.

'Hands up,' said the bush.

The barrel of a rifle jutted from amongst the branches and waved threateningly at her. Rosie decided to do as she was told but she couldn't help being curious.

'Excuse me, why are you dressed like a bush?' she asked.

'Mind your own business,' said the bush.

Rosie pulled a face. 'Can I put my hands down, please? I'm getting pins and needles.'

'Certainly not,' said the bush. The rifle jerked once more. 'Now step down. And no tricks, please, or it will be the worse for you.'

Still holding her hands high Rosie clambered down from the carriage.

She was about to ask another question when the bush began to move towards her in a rather ungainly, rolling fashion until it stopped about three paces from her. Then suddenly pitched forward with a crash to reveal a bespectacled boy of about her own age. His face was unnaturally pale and he was dressed in a thick woollen khaki soldier's uniform and wore boots and leggings. His dark eyes looked her up and down as though she was a horse that he was considering buying. He wrinkled his nose and his spectacles moved up. 'You're a girl,' he said disparagingly.

31

'I know that,' said Rosie.

'Then why are you wearing those things?' He pointed the rifle at her legs.

'What things?'

'Trousers.'

'They're not trousers, they're jeans. All the girls wear them where I come from.'

'Then all I can say is that you must come from a very strange place,' said the boy.

He walked round her slowly making Rosie feel very uncomfortable. He poked the gun into her back. 'I bet *they* sent you, didn't they?'

'Who?'

'You know very well. Old One-Eye and Bridey.'

'Never heard of them,' said Rosie.

He peered into her face smiling. 'Well, I don't believe you. And if you tell them you found me here it'll be the worse for you, I can tell you.'

'What d'you mean by worse exactly?' asked Rosie.

'You'll get shot,' said the boy clicking the rifle's hammer back.

'I won't tell,' said Rosie, who was all in favour of truth and heroism but on balance thought life was better. They looked at one another in silence for a few moments.

Rosie said, 'My arms are going to drop off soon. The blood's running out.'

The boy said, 'You can put them down when you've answered my questions.'

'I can't answer with my arms in the air,' said Rosie.

'Why not?'

'I just can't, that's all,' Rosie snapped. 'They're going to wither in a minute. I can feel it.'

She was thinking, I don't like this boy very much with his silly gun and silly uniform and that way of talking; more like an old professor than a twelve-year-old-boy. But it didn't seem wise to say all this while a gun was pointed at her so she remained diplomatically silent.

'I think I'm going to faint,' she said.

'Very well,' said the boy, 'you can put your arms down, only promise not to try to escape.'

32

Rosie promised. She lowered her arms and rubbed the life back into them.

He was looking at her fixedly. Rosie thought there must have been something wrong. 'What? What is it? Why are you staring?' She passed her hand over her face.

He stretched out his hand and took the scarf from her. He ran the length of it through his hands. 'Where did you get this?'

'I found it. Why?'

'Found? Where?'

Rosie pointed behind her. 'Back there somewhere. Why?'

'It's Aurora's.'

'Who?'

'My sister. I think she's been captured by enemy forces. Or maybe a witch.'

'A witch!' said Rosie.

'So I heard. But Aurora's always making up stories. That's why I like her. I've been looking for ages. I'm pretty good at tracking but I can't find a sign of her.'

He looked at her sternly, pointing his rifle. Rosie retreated until her back struck a tree. 'I think you've kidnapped her. You've got the look of a kidnapper.'

'What d'you mean?'

'Well, you look the type who'd do that sort of thing. Wearing trousers and so forth. The scarf proves it. It's what we call incriminating evidence. Now tell me where you're keeping her?'

'I've told you. I'm not keeping her anywhere. I just sort of found it.'

'Found? Don't lie. You took it. You kidnapped her and were coming to demand a ransom.'

'Don't you call me a liar.' She cast her mind back to the chase in the wood. 'I thought it was a game. Hide and Seek. She had taken something from me.'

'Taken? What?'

'Diary. My diary. She ran off with it. I thought it was just a game. Then I saw her hiding. Or thought I saw her. But when I got there there was just the scarf hanging in the tree.'

'Where is she now?'

'I don't know. She just sort of disappeared into thin air like a ghost. And then I couldn't find my way out. And then you came out dressed as a bush and here I am.' It was a long speech and it had all come tumbling out breathlessly. There was a silence. The boy looked at her, his head cocked to one side.

He doesn't believe me, Rosie thought.

'Oh dear,' said the boy brushing his hair back. 'Oh dear, oh dear, oh dear.'

'What's the matter?' Rosie asked.

'I'm afraid it's a court martial for you.'

'Court martial?' said Rosie. 'What's that?'

'It's a sort of trial we have in the army when someone's committed a crime.'

'What happens?'

'It's jolly interesting actually. You get asked a lot of questions and then you get shot.'

'But I haven't done anything wrong,' said Rosie. 'I'm telling the truth.'

The boy smiled loftily. 'The jury will decide that.'

'Who's the jury?'

'Me,' said the boy. 'Now, tell the court your name.'

'Rosie,' said Rosie.

'Rosie what? What rank are you? Captain? Infantry?'

'Just Rosie,' said Rosie.

'Second name?'

'Rosie . . . '

She stopped. No name would come to her lips.

'Second name?' repeated the boy.

Rosie shook her head. She thought desperately. Where had her name gone. She racked her memory. It was no use. 'I . . . I can't remember,' she confessed weakly.

The boy sighed deeply. 'Well, it doesn't look well for you so far. These are the easy questions. I'll give you one last chance. Where do you live?'

'At . . . ' Again nothing came to her. She began to shake.

'I suppose you can't remember that, either?'

'No,' said Rosie.

'You're lying. That means you're guilty. That's good. Now I'll get the judge to address the court.'

'Who's the judge?' asked Rosie.

'Me, of course,' said the boy.

'Well, I think that's stupid. How can you have a fair trial when you're everybody.'

'Don't you dare talk to the judge like that. Contempt of court. That's just to begin with. Then there's stealing the scarf. Attempting to steal my horse. Withholding information. Spying and, worst of all, wearing trousers. I'm afraid that's a capital offence. Do you want a handkerchief?'

'What for?'

'To put over your eyes when you get shot by the firing squad. Some do, you know.'

'What firing squad?' asked Rosie looking round.

'That's me as well,' said the boy cocking the rifle. 'Prisoner at the bar, have you anything to say?'

Rosie drew herself up. 'Yes, I have. I . . . '

'That's enough,' said the boy. He pointed the rifle at her. 'I hope you're going to die bravely. Ready, after three.'

'But you can't.'

'One, two . . . '

Suddenly the self pity seemed to flood out through one door and anger entered through another filling her to the brim. 'You're not going to shoot me.' She strode towards the boy. 'Anyway, that gun's not real.'

'Three.'

There was a sudden crack. Rosie gasped. Her body jerked. For a few seconds she did not move. Then she opened her eyes and felt her body for bullet holes. She seemed to be all there. The gun had fired a blank. She was still alive.

She turned on the boy. She'd show him. Who did he think he was? Her face and lips were white with fury. 'Give me that,' she shouted and wrenched the rifle from him. But he seized it back. His face was red with anger.

'Listen, you, you're supposed to be jolly well dead.'

'Well, I don't feel like it,' Rosie screamed back. She tugged the rifle. They stood toe to toe screaming at one another and pulling the rifle like a cracker that wouldn't burst.

'If you don't be dead I'll . . . I'll . . . shoot you.'

Rosie's anger lent her strength. She suddenly wrenched the gun out of his hands and flung it in a wide arc into the air. It crashed noisily into a clump of brambles at the edge of a shallow pond. The boy gazed from Rosie to the bushes and back again. His mouth opened and closed like a stranded goldfish but no sound came out. Rosie smacked her hands together.

'There. That'll teach you.'

The boy stepped towards her. 'All right. Trial of strength. It's your last chance. Bare-fisted combat. If you win that means you're telling the truth.'

Furiously he unbuttoned his tunic and flung it to the ground. He rolled up his shirt sleeves and stuck his left fist straight out in front of him. The other he tucked under his chin. 'Come on, put them up!' He began to dance round her on the balls of his feet, his back straight as a ram rod. 'I'd better warn you, I'm the best boxer in my school so you'd better look out. I'll give you one more chance to give in before I start. If you refuse it will be your own fault if you get hurt. Can't be fairer than that. What d'you say?'

'Look, I don't want to fight,' said Rosie. She turned in a circle, her eyes glued to him, waiting for his attack.

'You have no choice. Take the coward's way if you like. It'll do you no good. I'll give you a damned thrashing anyway.'

'But . . . ' began Rosie.

'No buts. You should have thought about that before you took my gun away. Too late now. Marquess of Queensberry rules, no mercy. No surrender. To the death. Ready?'

Rosie truly didn't want to fight but she had no choice. The boy rushed at her stiff legged and upright his left fist pumping in and out. She dropped into her judo crouch. He stopped, nonplussed at this. Then he laughed. 'I say, I can see you haven't done much boxing before. Would you like me to give you a few lessons first so as to make it worth my while?'

'No thanks,' said Rosie, turning, her eyes fixed on the boy.

'Well, don't say I didn't warn you.' He took up his stance again. 'Better watch out, here I come!'

And he suddenly lunged forward his left arm working in and out like a steam hammer. Rosie watched him like a hawk and as soon as he came within touching distance she grabbed his left wrist in her two hands and throwing herself sideways took the boy with her. His legs twisted round each other and he rolled over and over on the ground. Rosie bounced to her feet ready for

36

the next attack. The boy sat on the grass rubbing his head. He looked about him in a dazed sort of way.

'What happened?' he said. His eyes found difficulty focusing.

Rosie didn't really want to go on fighting. 'If you'd like to give in we could stop,' she said.

He staggered to his feet and stumbled about the clearing. 'Round two,' he said. 'It was just a lucky blow. Now I'm going to really teach you a lesson.' And once more he flung himself at her.

This time he flew rather higher. He had time for one short yelp of surprise before he hit the edge of the pond and slid slowly, face down into the water. Rosie jumped to her feet ready for the next attack. But the boy didn't move. His arms were spread-eagled and his head and shoulders were under the water.

'Oh God, he's drowning,' Rosie cried and sliding down the mossy bank she dragged the boy on to dry land. She turned him over. His face flopped sideways, mouth open.

'He's stopped breathing!'

She tried to remember what she had been taught about artificial respiration.

'Come on, you. Don't go and drown. Come on, come on.'

She turned him on to his stomach and began to press hard into his back. A spurt of water emerged from his mouth. To her relief she heard a faint gargling sound and redoubled her efforts. The gurgling became louder.

'That's good. Come on breathe, breathe,' she urged. The boy's back began to heave. Rosie turned him over. He was laughing. He clutched his stomach with both hands and began to roll about on the ground laughing uncontrollably.

'You rotten thing,' said Rosie. She began to pummel him about the body and shoulders. 'How dare you. You were pretending. All the time I was trying to save your life and you were laughing at me.'

But she found she couldn't be angry any more. She suddenly saw how funny it was. But she kept the laugh down. The boy rolled over and sat up facing her. 'Well, you cheated too. Fighting in that funny way.'

'That's judo,' said Rosie. 'That's not funny.' She began to laugh. 'It's not funny at all.'

Now they were laughing together. They rolled about on the

37

forest floor helpless and aching with laughter. At last they could laugh no more. They lay on their backs gasping for breath staring up at the branches.

The boy said, 'Rosie.'

'Yes.'

'My name's Alastair.'

He stuck out his hand and they shook.

'Alastair,' repeated Rosie.

He turned over and looked at her. 'Would you like another fight or would you prefer sandwiches and cake and lemonade?'

At the mention of food Rosie suddenly realized how hungry she was. 'Food, please,' she said.

He looked disappointed. 'We can fight after if you like.'

Alastair climbed up into the cart and brought down the bottle and a damp napkin. Inside were sandwiches and a large slice of cake. They leaned side by side against the wheel of the cart in a shaft of light and divided the sandwiches while the birds sang overhead and a soft wind swayed through the topmost branches of the trees.

And in another part of the forest a tall figure in a dark cloak heard the echo of the distant laughter and smiled to herself. She flung the spade to the shorter figure by her side. 'Dig,' she ordered in a soft whisper and raised her head and sniffed the breeze. 'They're close. Very close. Dig a nice deep hole for the two of them.'

5

It was the best lemonade Rosie had ever tasted. She tilted the bottle and felt the cooling bubbles slide down her throat. She wondered who had made it but there was no label on the bottle. She dreaded this strange boy with his superior voice finding out about her loss of memory. If she had known him well it would have been different. If he asked her any questions she decided she would lie. To make conversation she said, 'Did your mother make the lemonade?'

He exploded with laughter, sending lemonade spraying over the grass. He wiped his mouth on his hand.

'What's so funny?'

'Mother!' he snorted. 'Make lemonade!' The very thought set him off into more laughter. 'Cook made it, of course.'

'Oh, of course,' said Rosie as if it was the most natural thing in the world.

'Cook's famous for her lemonade. What's your cook like?'

'Oh, all right,' lied Rosie.

'Mother says we're lucky to still have her because of the war. I expect your mother has the same trouble.'

Rosie doubted it. She tried to picture her house and a woman moving in it who might be her mother. But there was nothing. An awful emptiness settled on her spirits. And yet she daren't risk Alastair's scorn.

'Well? Does she?' Alastair repeated.

'Pardon?'

'Your mother, does she have trouble getting servants?'

'Oh yes,' said Rosie. 'Yes she does. Heaps of trouble.'

The boy nodded agreement. 'It's the war,' he said solemnly.

'Ah yes, the war,' Rosie said nodding in agreement. She wondered what war he was talking about but thought it best not to enquire.

'It's getting the men to look after the estate. That's the difficulty.'

Rosie agreed once more. Large estates could be a burden.

'How many did you have?' asked Alastair.

'How many?'

'Yes. Servants? Before the war?'

She wondered what would be a reasonable number. Somewhere between one and ten perhaps. 'Oh . . . er . . . five.'

'Five?'

'Er . . . six,' she said carelessly with a wave of her hand.

Alastair looked at her. 'Six!' he said.

' . . . teen.' said Rosie swiftly. 'Sixteen.'

That seemed to satisfy him. 'Wasn't that funny my thinking you were sent to spy on me by Old One-Eye.'

'A hoot,' said Rosie.

'Where did you come from?'

'Come from?'

'Yes, where do you live?'

Rosie waved her arm and pointed vaguely. 'Over there.'

'Oh, towards the Beacons.'

'Yes.'

He took a bite of the sandwich and chewed for a moment staring straight ahead. 'There's only William and George left now. And George is seventy-five so he can't do much round the estate.'

'Sorry?'

'On the estate. Old servants can't do much really.'

Rosie agreed. She wished he'd change the subject away from servants and people she knew nothing about.

'You heard about William?'

'William?'

'Lost an eye. At the Somme. That's why we call him Old One-Eye. Not to his face, of course.'

'Of course not,' said Rosie.

'He's mother's chauffeur now.'

Rosie tried closing one eye and holding an imaginary steering wheel. 'Isn't it dangerous? Driving with one eye?'

'I suppose so,' said Alastair. 'Can't see a dicky bird on the right side. Has to have someone with him to warn him when there's something coming. "Look out, William, cow on the starboard bow." That sort of thing. I used to go with him. He'd even let me

40

drive sometimes. But now Bridey goes. She's the upstairs maid. I heard cook saying they're in love.' He leaned to her confidentially. 'Saw them kissing each other once when they thought no one could see but I jolly well could. It was frightful. Imagine doing that with your face to somebody else. Utterly beastly. Felt quite sick. They're supposed to keep an eye on me if my sister's not about but now they're spooning all the time it's easy to give them the slip. One-Eye used to be father's batman. I suppose your father's out there too, isn't he?'

'Out there?' Rosie wondered what he was talking about. 'Oh yes, he's out there all right,' she said.

'My father's in the Gloucesters. What regiment's yours with?'

Rosie wished he'd stop asking questions. She took another slice of cake to give her time to think. 'Oh, mine's in the Gloucesters too.'

'They're the best.'

'Definitely the best,' agreed Rosie.

For a moment they sat in silence then Alastair suddenly took a ribbon from about his neck. On the end was tied a bronze cross. He handed it to Rosie. It felt heavy in her palm. On one side was written 'For Valour' and on the other the name Brigadier R. L. T. Fenton.

'My grandfather won it in India. He gave it to me as a memento. I don't wear it, of course. That would be wrong.' From his pocket he took out a silver watch and flipped open the case. 'This is his as well.'

He slapped his forehead. 'Nearly seven. I'm going to be fearfully late. Look, I'm going to have to go. I'll be late for tea and then there'll be a row.'

'What about your sister?'

'Oh, she'll have gone back on her own, I expect.'

'You don't think anything's happened to her?'

He stood up. 'No. She'll be there waiting for me.'

Suddenly he took her hand and shook it vigorously. 'I enjoyed the fight, Rosie. Perhaps we could meet later in the week and have another one.'

'Thank you for the lemonade.'

'Don't mench.'

He packed the remains of the picnic into the haversack and

41

leapt on to the carriage. He turned and saluted her. 'Till we meet once more on the scene of battle,' he declared in a loud voice. 'And repledge ourselves to duty, heroism, and honour.'

Rosie felt rather silly but she thought it best to salute back. From the back of the carriage he took a blue flag and ran it up a small pole at the back of the dog cart. It fluttered against the dark trees. 'Regimental banner,' he called. Then, his hand cupped about his mouth he played the Last Post with his lips. The echoes died plaintively amongst the showering leaves. 'For old comrades hid in death's dateless night,' he explained. 'May they never be forgotten. Can I give you a lift?'

Rosie longed to tell him the truth.

'No, it's all right.'

'Just as you like.' He picked up the reins and shook them across the old pony's broad back.

The thought of being left alone in the forest filled her with dread. She ran towards him. 'Alastair?'

He turned to her. 'Yes.'

'Oh, nothing.' She ran towards a tangle of bushes and drew out the rifle. 'You forgot your gun,' she said.

He took it from her and holding it aloft shouted, 'Charge!' The old pony looked round at him. 'Come on, Ned. Charge, old boy.' Reluctantly the pony plodded across the clearing at his own steady pace. Rosie wanted to stop him; to say, 'Don't go. Help me! It was all lies that I said. I really can't remember who I am. Please help me.'

But the words stuck in her throat.

Where the lane turned Alastair looked back and waved. 'Farewell. Till we meet again.'

As he disappeared she heard him say to the pony, 'Buck up, Ned, or we'll be late for supper.'

For a second Rosie hesitated. The forest loomed above her and the night creatures were beginning to emerge. She shivered. She could hear Alastair singing loudly.

'Alastair,' she shouted and ran after him down the track. 'Wait, Alastair. I've something to tell you.'

6

'What, nothing! You can't remember anything at all?'

'Nothing,' said Rosie.

She sat beside him in the small cart staring at the ground through the floorboards. She couldn't bring herself to look at him. She felt so ashamed. It was a terrible thing, she thought. The very worst thing. Being nobody. Just Rosie No-Name.

'I thought it was a game,' he said at last. 'When you said you couldn't remember your name I thought you were pretending to be a spy.'

'No game,' Rosie said.

She glanced at him for a moment then turned away once more. The old pony reached up into a low branch and plucked a mouthful of leaves. Alastair pushed back the lock of dark hair that kept falling across his brow. 'And you can't remember where you live or anything.'

'Nothing.'

Alastair's face brightened. 'D'you know I've never met anybody who lost their memory before.'

'Well, don't sound so pleased about it,' she snapped. The way he said it made her sound like a freak or a performing seal. 'You wouldn't like it if it was you.'

'You're right,' he said. 'You know what we must do is to try and think of a way of getting it back.'

He leapt off the cart and began to pace backwards and forwards deep in thought.

Suddenly he clapped his hands together. 'Got it,' he exclaimed. He leapt back on to the cart. 'Remember William?'

Rosie nodded. 'One-eyed chauffeur who kept running over cows.'

'That's the one. Now, he told me once about this soldier he met in France. He lost his memory. Got kicked by a wayward mule. Just wandered about like you. Couldn't remember a thing. Life went to pieces. One day had a fight in a booth in a fairground and this bruiser punched him. Knocked him clean out. Bang! When he came round everything came back.'

Rosie shook her head in bewilderment. 'What's that got to do with me?'

'Don't you see. A bang knocked his memory out and then a bang brought it back.'

'So?'

'Well, we could do the same.'

'I'm not going to be punched in a boxing booth.'

'No, I was thinking why don't I give you a punch in the head. See what happens.'

'I'm not having you punch me in the head,' said Rosie.

'Not even a little punch?'

'Not even a little one,' said Rosie.

Alastair looked disappointed. 'Pity,' he said. He frowned and rested his head in both hands. 'Let's have another think.'

For a few moments there was silence. Suddenly he clicked his fingers. 'Elementary, my dear Rosie.'

She looked at him blankly. 'What is?'

'Why, Sherlock Holmes, of course.'

'That's not my name,' said Rosie.

'I know that. Haven't you ever heard of Sherlock Holmes?'

Rosie frowned. 'Wasn't he a detective in a book?'

'That's him. Solved crimes all over the place. Brilliant brain. Absolutely fearless. Just the sort of chap you need in a tight spot like this.'

Rosie looked at him. 'Alastair, how's a detective in a book going to help me get my memory back?'

'He can't. But there's nothing to stop us using his methods.'

'Methods?'

'Absolutely. Now, if he was here he'd be looking for clues.'

'Clues? Where?'

'Well, anywhere.' He looked her up and down. 'Why not start with your pockets.'

'Pockets?'

'Yes, empty them out. There might be something with your name on.'

He was right. Why hadn't she thought of that before. She searched through her jeans and pulled out a crumpled piece of lined paper. He took it from her and studied it. 'Awful writing,' he said. He put his spectacles on. 'Seems to be a list. What does this say? Wait a minute. I've got it. Edwards!'

'What?'

'Edwards. It must be your name.' He smiled broadly. 'There, bull's eye. Got it first time. I told you Sherlock Holmes would help.'

'Except that it's not my name.'

''Course it is,' said Alastair.

'Don't tell me what my name is.'

'If it's not your name why have you got Edwards written on a piece of paper in your pocket.'

Rosie shrugged. 'I don't know. But it's not my name.'

'How d'you know?'

'Well, I may not know what it is but I know what it isn't.'

'Mmm!'

He peered at the paper once more. 'How about Onion?'

'Definitely not.'

'Or Colli?'

Rosie shook her head.

'Haven't got a dog, have you? Collie dog. Try and think of his name.'

'Vegetable,' said Rosie suddenly.

'Vegetable? Funny name for a dog.'

'No, no,' said Rosie, 'that's what they are. Vegetables. Edwards, that's a sort of potato, cauli's short for cauliflower. And an onion is, well, it's an onion. It's a shopping list.'

Alastair looked disappointed.

'Any more brilliant ideas?' said Rosie.

'Well, at least I had an idea which is more than you've had. It's no good sitting about looking tragic.'

'You'd look tragic too if you didn't know who you were.'

He jumped down from the carriage. 'I'm going to walk about a little,' he said.

'Are you upset?'

'Not upset,' he said without pausing. 'Don't get upset. It's one of my best points. Walking helps the brain.'

She watched him walking briskly up and down murmuring to himself. She climbed down from the carriage and put her arms

45

about the old pony's neck for comfort. 'Bet you know who you are, don't you, Ned?'

Ned stared at her and carried on chewing. She stroked his nose gently.

'Clothes!' cried Alastair suddenly.

'Clothes?'

'Yes. Don't you see. You're bound to have a label with your name on. Like a dog. You know—"My name is Fido. Please take me back to my owner". That sort of thing.'

'I'm not a dog,' snapped Rosie.

'No, but you're lost.' He pulled at her collar. 'Look, here's a label.'

'What does it say?'

Alastair sqinnied at the label. 'St Michael. It says Saint Michael.'

'Rosie St Michael,' Rosie whispered. 'No, doesn't sound right.'

'Better than Rosie Cauliflower anyway,' said Alastair. He looked again. 'Wait, there's something else. It says—"Hand wash in lukewarm water".'

'That's not much help,' said Rosie.

He sighed. 'Well, I can't think of anything else.' He looked up at the sky. 'It's going to be dark soon. The best thing is if you come home with me.'

'Will I have to tell everybody?'

'Of course.'

Trouble is, she thought to herself, there's nothing to tell. But he was right. There was nothing else for it. It would be embarrassing but it was the only thing to do. She didn't really look forward to going to Alastair's house with the mother who never cooked or worked and even had someone to dress her in the morning, the cook and the maids and the one-eyed chauffeur. But anything was better than spending the night in the forest. 'All right,' she said.

Suddenly Ned gave a squeal and lurched forward so suddenly that Rosie staggered.

'What did you do?' asked Alastair.

'Nothing,' said Rosie. 'I was just standing there and he leapt into the air.'

The pony was pawing the earth, his eyes rolling. Foam frothed at his nostrils. He rolled agitatedly from side to side and suddenly reared up kicking out with his front hooves.

Alastair held the harness and stroked him gently, whispering in his ear. 'Steady, Ned. Steady, old boy.' He turned to Rosie. 'Something's frightened him.'

But Rosie wasn't listening. She was wondering why her body was shaking. At first she thought it was the cold. But the evening was warm. Then she realized it was not her but the ground itself that shook. A distant roaring filled her ears; like drums beating. Could it be an earthquake?

'Listen,' said Alastair.

'I know,' said Rosie.

The noise came nearer. Ned's hooves pawed the air. He reared forward dragging the carriage behind him. The left wheel leapt spinning into the air and struck Rosie on the back hurling her to the ground. Alastair was shouting at the terrified pony trying to hold him back. But he broke free and galloped off the track down a slope, the carriage bouncing crazily behind him flinging its contents to the ground.

Rosie lay on the ground. Her ears were full of drumming. She shook her head, trying to clear it. She thought the earth would split open.

Then she heard Alastair screaming at her. 'Rosie! Look out! Look out!'

Then she saw him, gleaming through the dark trees. A huge black stallion, his hooves flashing like blades, towing behind him a black carriage. Down he bore on her, nostrils gaping. His hooves beat like thunder. And in his eyes the devil's own fire.

7

'Rosie!' screamed Alastair.

She rolled herself across the lane and down the bank. Thunder filled her ears. The stallion was lathered with sweat. The carriage swayed and jolted crazily, dust pouring from the bounding wheels like smoke. For an instant, a gloved hand emerged from a small window. For a moment she thought the occupant was waving. But then something white fluttered into the air. Caught by the wind it soared. Then another and another until the air was thick with large flat snowflakes that drifted earthwards in the wake of the carriage. A thick pall of dust descended on them. Rosie laid her head on the soft earth of the forest.

When the last sound had died Rosie raised her head. The lane was empty. A film of dust powdered the grass and the trees. She tried to rise but suddenly felt immensely tired, drained and weary. She could hear Alastair's voice talking to Ned, calming him down. Then he was shouting her name. He sounded far away. Like a voice in a dream. How tired and heavy her eyes felt. She closed them. Someone shook her.

'Get up,' Alastair shouted.

'Leave me alone,' she murmured thickly.

'Rosie, what's the matter? Are you ill? Did you hurt yourself?'

It was as though he was speaking from miles away down a long tunnel.

She tried to push herself upright but her arms had lost their strength. She wondered if she was ill. Alastair began to shake her. She forced her tired eyes open. About her the ferns and the grass looked strangely huge; at once very close and yet far away. In a half sleep she studied the leaves and the blades of grass as though she had never seen them before. It was strange how the grass was yellow and withered where only a moment earlier it had been a vibrant green. She noticed a wild flower. Its head hung, ragged and blackened.

A thin triangular thing was growing out of her forearm. She

48

studied it; like a tiny ship with dark sails becalmed on her arm. She was about to brush it off when she realized it was a butterfly. 'Red Admirable,' she slurred, her tongue half asleep. She plucked him up gently between thumb and forefinger and held it in her open palm. 'Fly away, fly away.' But the butterfly toppled over on to its side. Dead, she thought sadly. Poor dead butterfly. Poor dead admiral.

Alastair pulled at her roughly. She flapped at him with her arm. 'Go 'way,' she said petulantly. 'Leave me alone. Sleep. Want to sleep.'

'You mustn't sleep,' Alastair cried urgently.

She tried to fight him off but she was too weak. He pulled her to her knees and held her there swaying backwards and forwards. Her head lolled. No matter how she tried her eyes kept closing. She cried out as something splashed about her face blinding her. A sweet taste. She ran her tongue across her lips. Alastair was standing above her, the lemonade bottle in his hand. Her face and hair were drenched. What a waste of good lemonade, she thought. But she felt more awake. He gripped her arms and heaved her to her feet. She almost fell but he bore her up.

'Walk,' he instructed.

'Walk yourself, bossy boots.'

She saw something on the grass at her feet. 'Mind!' she shouted.

'What is it?'

'There.' She pointed.

'Dead sparrow,' said Alastair.

She felt angry suddenly and stamped her foot. 'Not dead,' she shouted. She bent to pick it up, cradling it in both palms. Its head lolled. Alastair was right. 'Poor, poor sparrow,' she murmured. She felt a tremendous sorrow in her. The little bedraggled creature lay on its back, tiny legs pointing at the sky. She was thinking, how huge the sky was and how thin and fragile the sparrow's legs. And yet they both lived in the same great world. Gently she laid him down and rubbed her heavy lids.

'Look there. And there!' Alastair pointed. A host of sparrows littered the ground as though they had fallen out of the sky like so many stones. 'All dead,' said Alastair.

'What's happened?' Rosie asked.

49

Alastair shook his head. 'I don't know.'

She clutched his arm hard, looking up the lane where she had last seen the carriage and the huge stallion.

'Whoever was in the carriage did it.'

He laughed. 'Don't be silly.'

'Then what?'

'You must have banged your head again.'

She felt her head gently. There was no bump nor scar. She began to droop once more.

'Come on, walk,' he ordered. She tottered along leaning heavily on his arm.

'Sing,' he said.

'Sing?'

'Anything. To keep you awake.'

'I don't know any songs.'

He began to sing in a strident, tuneless voice.

'Onward Christian soldiers
Marching as to war.'

'Come on, join in.'

She raised her voice. It was strange she could remember the words of the song. How was it she could remember the song but not her own mother and father?

'Sing!'

'With the cross of Jesus
Marching on before.'

'Louder!' he commanded.

And they sang as loudly as they could, keeping step to the rhythm, their shrill voices ascending through the branches to the unseen sky beyond. The old pony turned his head and pricked his ears.

'Are you awake now?'

'I think so.'

Alastair let her go. She swayed a little but remained standing. 'I was wondering,' he said. 'The soldier in the boxing booth.'

She frowned. What was he on about?

'You know. One blow knocked out his memory. The next brought it back. Might have happened to you.'

She leaned on a tree, her head down. But still the memories wouldn't come.

50

'Nothing?'

She shook her head sadly. 'No,' she said.

She began to slide down the trunk of the tree. He gripped her roughly and, shouting, he walked her briskly back and forth once more.

She said, 'I'm fine, leave me alone.'

But as soon as he released her she began to crumple towards the ground. He held her by the shoulder and slapped her stingingly across the face. That woke her. She stared at him angrily. 'What d'you want to do that for?' She drew back her hand and slapped him back. He staggered. She covered her face expecting a blow but he was laughing.

'That's woken you up.'

It was true. The anger had jolted her into wakefulness, not the blow. The strength began to seep back into her limbs. She ran her fingers through her hair. Inhaled deeply.

'Better?' he said.

She wasn't sure how she felt. 'What happened, Alastair?'

'You sort of fainted.'

She shook her head. 'I did not faint. I never faint.'

She looked up towards the lane. 'It was that carriage. That black horse. That's what did it.' She looked about her, fearful that it might return. 'Let's get away from here.'

He laughed. 'It wasn't the carriage. You banged yourself as you fell.'

'Well, what about the dead birds? The butterfly? The flowers?'

He shrugged. 'There's probably a logical explanation,' he said.

She asked for the lemonade. He handed her the bottle and she drank the few remaining drops.

'You look like death,' he said.

'Thanks a bunch,' she said flatly. 'I feel like death.'

He gave one of his coughs. 'We could sing again if you like.'

'No thanks.'

'Or I could tell you a joke. Listen. Teacher to boy . . . '

'Not just now,' she said.

He helped her into the carriage and wrapped a blanket about her. Then they climbed the shallow slope back up to the track. She plucked at his sleeve. 'Not this way.'

'What d'you mean?'

51

'This is the way the black horse and carriage went.'

'I know.'

'We mustn't go this way.'

'Why not?'

She paused. 'I don't know. It frightens me. It's an intuition and I'm never wrong. Please turn back.'

'Can't, this is the way home.'

He clicked his tongue and slapped the reins on Ned's back. 'Might even catch them if we hurry. Find out who it was?'

'No!' If only she didn't feel so weak.

The carriage stopped. She thought, Thank goodness, he's turning round. But he had leapt down from the carriage and was running up the road. 'Look, Rosie!'

He waved something in the air.

'What is it?'

'Don't know,' he shouted. 'Blank paper. There's a date though. Today's date.' He looked about. 'Here's another and another.' He picked them up and ran back to the carriage. His face was alive with excitement and curiosity. It's all a game to him, Rosie thought. All life is one big pretend.

'What does it mean?' he asked.

She took the papers from him, recognizing them right away. The pages were blank.

'My diary.'

'Yours? Are you sure?'

'Of course I'm sure,' she said. 'I always have a year of empty pages. It's my diary, I'd know it blindfold.'

He looked up at her. 'But didn't you say Aurora had taken it?'

She nodded.

'Then that means . . . '

They looked at one another then up the track which lay still and tranquil before them.

'She must have been in the carriage. Pity it doesn't say anything.' He looked about him. 'Wait a minute.'

Before she could stop him he was running about the lane picking up the other sheets. He brought them back. She leafed through them. They were all blank.

'Here's something.'

She took the sheet from him. The page was labelled 'Today'.

At the bottom one word was written in black spidery writing.

'What is it?' he asked.

She didn't answer.

'What's the matter?'

'My name,' whispered Rosie. 'It says my name.'

He took the paper from her.

'Pity you didn't write your second name,' he said. 'Or your address.'

She shook her head slowly. 'Not my writing.'

He didn't seem to notice how pale her face was.

He turned over the page. 'Wait, there's more.'

At the top of the page in the same handwriting was written, '*First Aurora. Then Rosie.*'

She seized him. Shook his shoulders. 'Oh, Alastair, turn round. It's a trap. I know it is.'

He was laughing. 'A trap. Don't be silly. It's Aurora. She saw she was going to be late home so one of our neighbours gave her a lift.'

'But why did she throw my diary out of the window?'

'To let us know she was there. She probably saw us. She's always doing things like that. It's just her way.'

'But the writing.'

His eyes suddenly widened. 'I know,' he said excitedly, 'it's a race. She wants us to race her. It means she's going to be first and we'll be second. Easy if you've got a bit of brain power. Come on. We'll show her.'

He leapt up into the carriage, seizing the reins. 'Come on, Ned. Full gallop.'

'No,' screamed Rosie. 'It's dangerous. I can't explain. I just know.'

She was shouting at him, beating at his back with her fists. 'We'll never catch them. Never.'

Suddenly he hauled on the reins and they lurched down from the track. She was thrown backwards in a heap into the rear of the carriage. Alastair guided the carriage on to a high grassy plateau. In the distance she could hear the sound of a waterfall. He turned, smiling. He was enjoying the race. 'I know a short cut,' he said. 'We'll beat her this way.'

They bumped and rolled along once more. She clung on to the

rails, jolted from side to side. She saw something square and red in the grass to her right. 'Alastair.'

'What?'

She pointed. 'Stop. Look.'

'What?'

'There! My diary.'

He stood up, pulling back on the reins. 'Whoa, boy!' and leapt down from the carriage. 'Wait here,' he said. 'Probably another message. She must have known this short cut as well.'

He slid down the slope picking up odd pages. 'Blank,' he shouted. 'Another blank.'

'Be careful.'

He was laughing now, picking up pages as he ran without stopping. 'Like a paper chase,' he shouted. 'Hare and hounds. And we're the hounds.'

But Rosie was thinking about her diary and how the papers had been scattered. Yes, it was a chase. But although they were doing the chasing, they were the victims. And she knew where they were being led. She knew it in her bones. She stood up and shouted with all her strength. 'Alastair, stop! It's a trap.'

But he was too far off to hear. She watched him running towards a small square of lighter grass. The diary lay just beyond it.

'Alastair!' she screamed. 'Alastair, stop!'

This time he heard her. Still running he turned and raised his hand, his face turned towards her, smiling. And then she saw the smile change. His eyes wide, his mouth open. The arm flung up in greeting now waved stupidly as though he were attempting to climb an invisible ladder in the air. There was a rush of grass and sticks breaking and falling. And he was gone from her and there was silence.

8

'Alastair!'

He lay crumpled at the bottom of the pit, not moving.

He shifted and groaned, turning his head to look up at her. His face was grey and knotted with pain. 'Never was much good at the long jump,' he said trying to smile. Leaning on the wall he tried to stand. He winced as he put his weight on his right leg.

'Alastair, are you all right?'

'It's my ankle,' he groaned, 'I think I've broken it.'

He sat down once more and removed his shoe. His right ankle was swollen.

'Wiggle your toes,' Rosie said.

'Pardon.'

'Wiggle your toes. I read about it somewhere. If you can wiggle your toes it means you haven't broken anything.'

He leaned his back against the wall of the pit. Stretched out his legs.

'Are they moving?'

'Yes.'

'It must be a sprain. Try to stand.'

He turned to face the wall and used his hands to lever himself upright. 'Ouch.' His face twisted with pain.

'Does it hurt?'

He forced a smile. 'Not really.'

'Don't be silly. It's no use trying to be brave if it hurts.'

'It hurts.' He gave a short laugh. 'Stupid thing to do. Fall down a hole like that.'

'It's not a hole, Alastair. Don't you see? Someone dug it.'

'Dug it?'

'On purpose. That's what the papers were for. And the diary. To lead you on. Or to lead me on.'

'But who would do that?'

Rosie shook her head. She was suddenly aware of the great expanse of dark forest at her back. Whoever had dug the pit was out there somewhere. Were they watching now? She had a sense that someone was standing just behind her. She wanted to look but somehow she was unable to turn her head. She heard a harsh breath. Something touched her arm. 'Aaaaaaagh!' She almost toppled into the pit.

'Rosie, what is it?'

She laughed. 'Nothing. I thought it was somebody but it was only Ned trying to get into my pocket.'

He laughed.

'What shall we do?'

'Let's have a think. My brain's all right. Good job I don't think with my ankle, though.'

He leaned back against the wall. Rosie was thinking, half an hour ago I didn't know Alastair existed. Then I didn't like him. Thought he was a pain. All that wanting to fight, his stupid uniform, his bad jokes, and that way he had of talking. But now she felt as though she had known him all her life.

'Rosie.'

'Yes?'

'I was just thinking.'

'What?'

'About you and me really. Well, since you can't remember anything that happened before this afternoon, it's as if your life has just started. And I'm the only person you've met. So I suppose in a way I'm your oldest chum.'

Chum, she thought. What a funny old-fashioned word. But she liked it. Chum, chum. She repeated it over to herself.

'What d'you think?' he asked.

'Yes, I suppose you are.'

'And Ned, of course.'

'Oh yes, and Ned. But he doesn't tell such good jokes as you.'

He laughed. 'That's very flattering. I say, would you like to hear another?'

'Not just now. We ought to think of how to get you out.'

'Absolutely right. Tell you what, Rosie. I'm just going to sit here for a minute. Why not have a look at your diary. I mean, I've already fallen into the trap so you might as well find out who you are.'

He was right. She walked round the pit. Even before she

56

picked up the little book though she knew what she would find. She walked back to the edge of the pit.

'Well? Don't keep me in suspense, Rosie. Who are you? Where d'you come from?'

She held up the leather-covered book. The covers flapped open. 'It's empty,' she said.

'Empty?'

'Whoever had it has taken all the pages.'

Neither of them spoke for a moment. Then he said, 'I'm sorry, Rosie. Rosie?'

'What?'

'I'm sure Row didn't do it. Take all the pages out. I mean, she likes a jape but she's not malicious. It must have been somebody in the carriage. How could they do that? Tear it up like that. It's like . . . like tearing up somebody's life and throwing it away.'

She was thinking the same thing. There was a silence. No birds sang. It was as though they were the only people left alive on earth.

He said softly, 'I say, Rosie. Are you all right?'

'Fine.'

'Sure? I could tell you a joke if you like.'

She didn't really want to hear it but she thought it might cheer him up. 'Go on, then.'

'It's a French verb. Do you know any French?'

'A bit.'

'It's the verb to laugh. Ready?' He began to recite very quickly, 'Je laugh, tu roar, il giggle, nous roarons, vous splittez, ils bust.'

It was quite funny. Alastair began to laugh. He laughed so much that he fell on his back and banged his ankle.

'Ouch!'

'Sssh!'

'What?'

'They may hear us.'

'Who?'

'Whoever dug the pit. They'll be back.'

They were whispering now.

She said, 'Do you think you could have a try at getting out?'

'Don't know. I'll try.'

He hauled himself painfully to his feet. 'There's a root here,' he said and jammed his good foot behind it. He searched for a hand hold but as he pulled himself up the root crumbled and he fell back with a cry of pain.

'Walls are too smooth,' he said.

Every minute Rosie expected a hand to fall on her shoulder. She didn't know whose. It was just a feeling. She knew from experience that these feelings were rarely wrong. She cast anxious glances behind her. The sun was fading. She said, 'Wait. I'll come down.'

'Don't be stupid. What's the point of both of us being down here.'

His voice had been angry. There was a silence.

'Rosie, you still there?'

'Of course. D'you think I'd leave you?'

She lay flat at the rim of the pit and extended her right hand. 'See if you can reach my hand,' she said.

'Oh, Rosie, it's too high.'

'Try!' she shouted. 'For goodness' sake try.'

He stretched upwards standing on the tip of one boot. Their hands were inches apart.

'Can't,' he said.

She stretched further.

'Be careful.'

Her shoulders were over the edge. 'Try harder.'

She felt the tips of his fingers. Like ice. Shaking. Then they clasped hands. She gripped hard locking her left hand over the wrist of her right.

'You can't do it. I'm too heavy,' he said. 'I'm going to let go.'

'Don't you dare,' she shouted. 'I'm going to pull. Ready after three.'

They counted together. On three she gave a cry and heaved with all her might. His foot left the ground. Then he was slipping back and she too was being dragged towards the edge. She tried to dig in with the points of her shoes but she was sliding helplessly. She was almost over when she felt him let go. She scrabbled at the crumbling brink trying to keep her legs down. She thought she was gone but at the last moment somehow she managed to throw her weight backwards. She lay on the ground for a moment panting, unable to speak.

58

She heard a strange sound. Like wind blowing through lou-vered blinds. A swift, breathy, chattering sound. She looked over the edge. Alastair was lying on the floor. His teeth rattled uncon-trollably. His whole body was shaking.

'Oh, Alastair, are you ill?'

'F-f-f-f-f-fine,' he managed to say. 'Just a bit cold.'

'It's not just the ankle, is it?'

'Chest hurts a bit.'

'You must keep warm.'

She ran to the cart and found the blanket. Inside it was an apple. She threw the blanket down. He wrapped it about himself. His teeth were still chattering. 'That's much better,' he said.

'Catch!' She lobbed the apple down.

'Aren't you hungry?'

'Listen,' she said. 'You may have cracked a rib. Don't move about.'

He looked about and up at her. 'I'm not going anywhere,' he said and laughed.

'I've just thought of something,' Rosie said. 'We're so stupid. We ought to use Ned. He's stronger than either of us. I can undo the reins and buckle them together. How do I get him out of his harness?'

'I'll explain. But whatever you do don't let him wander off. He'll go home.'

She stood up and stroked the old pony, whispering his name in soft tones. Then while Alastair shouted instructions she disman-tled his harness and led him out of the shafts of the cart. 'Done it. What do I do next?'

'Now unbuckle the reins. Then make one end fast to Ned's harness and lower the other end down to me.'

Ned stood patiently while she carried out the instructions.

Alastair gripped the end and tried to loop it about himself underneath both arms. But the reins weren't long enough. He tied the end about his elbow, jerking it tight. He looked up at her. His face was grey with pain.

'Now back him up.'

She took Ned's bridle. 'Come on, boy. Come on back.'

He stared at her then with a shake of his mane he took a step backwards. A cry came from the pit.

59

She moved to the rim of the pit. Both his feet were off the ground. 'You all right, Alastair?'

'A.l.' She could hear the pain in his voice. 'Keep on,' he said.

She urged Ned once more. He moved back a step. Then she saw the strap twisting in the buckle. Slowly the leather was shredding.

'Quick!'

She hauled at the pony. 'Come on, Ned.'

He took another step. She saw Alastair's fingers scrabbling in the mud at the pit's rim. 'Nearly there.'

'Two more steps, Ned. Come on.'

He took the first. There was a dull snapping sound. The pony and she stumbled backwards. She heard a cry and the thump of Alastair's body. She ran to the edge and knelt. He lay crumpled at the foot of the pit wall. The broken half of the rein still curled about his arm and wrist.

'Alastair!'

He rolled on to his side and on to his knees. His head hung down. Then he looked at her. 'I don't think that worked,' he whispered breathlessly. The shaking had started again.

'What shall we do now?' Rosie said.

His voice was fainter. 'Only one thing for it. You'll have to get help from home.'

'How? I don't know where I am.'

'Ned knows. Let him go his way and he'll take you there. If you say to him "Home, boy. Walk on" he'll find it on his own. I've often done it. Even fallen asleep sometimes and he's taken me home.'

'But the strap's broken.'

'Ride him.'

'Ride?'

'You have ridden a horse before?'

Rosie hesitated.

'Haven't you?'

'I don't know,' she said. 'I'll soon find out.'

'Try. He's very quiet.'

'OK,' she said. She stood up and brushed the mud from her.

'Rosie! I was just thinking. In case you get lost you ought to leave a trail.'

'I thought you said he knew his way.'

'He does. But just in case. In the cart there's a ball of string. Pay it out. Then if something happens at least you'll be able to find your way back here.'

She found the ball of string inside a small hinged wooden box. She stuffed it into her pocket.

'Did you find it?'

'Yes,' said Rosie.

'Give me the other end. If you're in trouble give it a tug.'

She fed the end of the string down to him. He tied it about his wrist. She tucked the ball into her jumper. She knew he wouldn't be able to feel the tug even if she did pull. And suppose she was in danger, what could he do to help, stuck as he was at the bottom of a pit with a twisted ankle. She was comforted nevertheless.

She walked up to the pony and took his long ears gently in her fists. Gazing into his large dark eyes she whispered, 'Listen, Ned. I'm a girl and you're a horse. I don't know if I've ever ridden one of you before. So just take it easy, OK. No galloping. No standing on your back legs. No jumping. Just get me to the house. It's worth a bowl of sugar lumps. Is it a deal?'

Ned looked at her unblinking. Rosie sighed. 'I don't think you understand a word I'm saying.'

'Rosie!'

She walked back to the pit. Alastair said, 'He'll take you to the ferry. There's a flat-bottomed boat. You have to turn a windlass. Have you seen one before?'

Something whispered in her memory. 'Somewhere,' she said.

'It's very easy. Just untie the rope and turn the windlass. It's stiff to start but once the boat's moving it's quite easy to keep it going. It'll take Ned as well. Then walk up the slope and you'll see the house.'

She hated to leave him. She looked down. He was smiling.

'I'm going now. Don't worry, I'll be back. Are you all right?'

He gestured round the muddy pit. 'I wouldn't want to be anywhere else.'

She wanted to laugh, to put her arms around him and hug him.

'Rosie. Stiff upper lip.'

'What does that mean?'

'I don't know really. It's something people say.'

'Can you still wiggle your toes?'

'Yes. Does that mean I'm alive?'

'It's a good sign.'

She walked over to Ned and looked at him. 'Listen, you. I'm going to climb on to your back so if you know what's good for you, stand still, mate.'

She put both hands on to his back and leapt. He gave a snort and backed away. Her hands clinging to his back she felt herself pulled towards him, the toes of her shoes dragging in the earth. 'Ned, stop that. Stop!' At last he did and speaking to him softly she led him by the bridle to the dog cart.

She pointed her finger. 'Stand there.'

Then she climbed into the cart and prepared to scramble on to his back. 'This time I mean it!' She wagged her finger. Ned chewed the snaffle showing his great yellow teeth. She looped both arms about his neck. 'One, two, three, jump,' she said to herself. Then she threw herself at him.

It wasn't a very good jump but she managed to get her right leg bent across his back. He shifted sideways. His back was much more slippery than she had imagined. Her left leg jerked in the air. She managed to get some purchase from the rail of the cart and shoved. Too hard. She almost pitched herself over on to the other side.

Rather surprised at having a human being balancing on his back like an ungainly sack of potatoes, Ned decided to go for a stroll. Head hanging down on one side, legs on the other Rosie bounced up and down.

'Whoa!' Rosie said. Ned began to canter in a circle. 'I said whoa not go,' said Rosie. She felt like a circus act gone wrong. With every step the breath was jolted out of her. She scrabbled desperately with her right leg.

'Everything all right?' Alastair shouted.

'Terrific,' said Rosie.

'I just knew you'd ridden before.'

'Me too,' said Rosie watching the ground bounce past her upside-down head.

'If you want him to stop you just shout, Easy, Ned.'

62

At the sound of his master's command Ned suddenly stopped. Slowly Rosie slid to the ground.

'Have you done it?' Alastair cried.

Rosie dusted herself down. 'No problem,' she said.

She led him back to the cart and mounted once more. This time she managed to get both legs astride.

Alastair shouted. 'Try to sit upright. Go with the rhythm. And don't make him gallop.'

'You must be joking,' said Rosie.

'Say home, boy. Walk on,' Alastair instructed.

Ned's ears pricked at the sound of his master's voice. He began to walk backwards towards the pit.

'Whoa,' Rosie screamed.

'What is it?'

'He's gone into reverse,' Rosie said.

'Give him a kick with your heels.'

She did so. To her surprise Ned stopped. She kicked once more. He took a step forward. Then another. 'Home, boy,' she said. 'Home.'

Head down at a leisurely pace he ambled out of the clearing.

'Rosie,' shouted Alastair.

'Can't stop now. Bye,' said Rosie.

'Good luck,' Alastair said.

Bouncing in the most ungainly fashion on the pony's back, Rosie walked Ned slowly out of the clearing past the dark pool and up a slight hill. She leaned forward and held on to his mane.

'Good boy, Ned. Walk on,' she whispered in his ear. 'Walk on home. And remember, no galloping.' She dug her heels in gently. 'Home, boy,' she whispered in his ear. 'Home.'

And as she said the word a wave of sadness swept through her.

9

A song kept running through Rosie's brain. She didn't know where it came from or why she kept singing it softly to herself. But back it kept coming.

> And the poor maid dressed in loneliness
> Rode through the Forest of Forgetfulness
> To the dark pool

What did it mean? She shook her head. It came from that unknown country that lay on the other side of her memory.

She wondered how long she had been riding? Twenty minutes? Half an hour? It was difficult to tell. Ned plodded forward, his head rising and falling, shoulders sliding forward. First the left then the right. 'You seem to know where you're going, Ned.'

She wished she'd asked Alastair how long it took to reach the river. All very well trusting a horse. But suppose he was going in completely the wrong direction. What then? Paying out the string, she wondered about turning round. But then she knew less about the forest than Ned did. She decided to count to two thousand. If the river hadn't appeared by then she would turn back. But round about one thousand she lost count.

Her mind began to wander. In her bright imagination she saw herself riding between the hedges of a large garden and then dismounting before seven broad steps that led to a porticoed doorway. A handsome woman ran down to meet her. 'Alastair,' she cried. 'Where is he? What's happened?'

'There it is. The river.'

She said it with such sharpness that Ned stopped. The woman, the garden, and the large imposing doorway drifted from her. The river! There it was shining between the trees; a gleam of flat water with the sun's last sparkle on it.

She patted Ned. 'Well done,' she cried. 'And to think I thought we were lost.'

She urged him on with a dig in the flanks. Her spirits suddenly rose. She rolled off the pony and ran down to the tiny jetty. There was something wrong. The boat, instead of nestling at the bank, lay in mid-stream.

Somebody forgot to tie it up properly, she thought and pulled the dripping rope from the stream. There was no weight to it. The end came to her hand. It must have rotted, she thought. But the end wasn't frayed, it was cut cleanly across. As though by a sharp knife. She gave a cry and dropped it as if it burnt her. Somebody had been here. Had cut the rope on purpose. To trap them.

Above her head she heard laughter. Acchchchchchchchc!

She turned. A large black bird swooped towards her. She covered her head instinctively. Felt the beat of the dark wings as he passed her. A terrified stuttering neigh.

'Ned!'

The bird descended, claws extended towards the pony. Ned's eyes rolled white. Up on to his hind legs he rose pawing the air with his front hooves. The bird raked across his head, stabbing at the eyes. Six tracks of red opened along the length of his muzzle. He screamed and twisted away shaking his mane and head.

She picked up a stick and ran towards him, beating at the savage bird. But the pony turned from her and galloped towards the forest.

'Ned. Stop. Come back,' Rosie cried and ran after him. But he was gone, his tiny hooves thundering into the darkness of the forest. She ran after him till she could run no more. She listened for the sound of his hooves but only a great silence descended upon her. Then a screech. Looking up she caught a glimpse of the bird climbing the sky. His screech like hard, cruel laughter rang above the tall trees.

'You!' she shouted at it. 'Look what you've done now.'

Then he too was gone and she was alone. There was no sound save that of her own breathing. She shouldn't have shouted but she couldn't help herself.

'Help,' she screamed. 'Heeeeeelp!'

But nobody replied.

She slumped down on the bank, her head in her hands. She thought of Alastair lying alone in the dark forest, waiting for her. She imagined his face dropping as she told him the news. She

65

imagined his scorn. *What, you let him get away? I warned you about that.* She hated the thought of telling him. But there was no alternative. Nothing for it but to go back the way she had come. She searched for the string and thought of his hand on the other end of it. It was comforting. She gave it a tug hoping he might answer but of course he was too far away and the string too loose.

And the poor maid dressed in loneliness
Walked the Forest of Forgetfulness
To the dark pool.

The words of the old song came to her once more.

Winding the string about her hand as she walked she climbed back up the slope and through the trees. She had an idea. They could double the string. Make it as thick as they could. Fix it to the cart wheel and then get Ned to pull . . . She stopped. She had forgotten. Ned was gone. She began to run, winding in the string in great loops.

At the glade with the dark pool her spirits rose. Thank goodness she had taken the string.

'Alastair!'

There was no reply.

Probably asleep, she thought and smiled. She fell to her knees at the edge of the pit.

She whispered, 'Alastair.'

The bruised, half-eaten apple lay abandoned. But of Alastair there was no sign. She closed her eyes in despair and disbelief. *Please God let him be there when I open them again.* But when she opened them again the pit was still empty. She was shivering but whether with fear or the cold breath of the approaching night she could not tell. She felt utterly abandoned and alone. Loneliness seemed to make her shrink as though the dark trees had grown taller and she somehow smaller.

It began to rain; a steady downpour that came straight down through the windless evening. She stood up and, heedless of the danger, cried out aloud, 'Alastair! Alastair!'

Now that she might never see him again she realized how much she cared for him. She promised herself that if they met again she would ask him to tell all his jokes one after the other and she would laugh like a drain.

'Alastair!'

She began to run hither and thither talking to herself. She was weeping now. Her tears mingled with the rain. Her hair lay flat and twisted on her head. Her jeans clung to her. The cold was in her bones. She didn't know why she was running but she couldn't stop herself. She wondered if she was going mad. She hoped desperately that it was a dream but she knew it wasn't. Then something made her stop in her tracks.

'Alastair!'

He was sitting wrapped in a blanket by the porch of a cottage. Relief swept through her. How clever of him to climb out of the pit on his own. She ran forward.

'Oh, Alastair. I'm so glad I've found you, Alastair. Why didn't you wait for me?'

She put both hands upon his shoulders.

The old woman turned and smiled up at her. Smiled up through black and broken teeth.

10

Rosie drew back, startled.

'I'm sorry, I thought you were . . . ' she stopped.

The old woman looked up at her from beneath her shawl.

'Thought?'

'You were somebody else.'

'Who would that be?'

Rosie wondered how much she should tell this old lady she had only just met but her twinkling eyes and sympathetic smile disarmed her.

'Alastair. I lost him. In the wood. I didn't know what to do. So I ran about looking and then I thought I saw him but it was you.'

Rosie wiped the rain from her face. The old woman looked up at her with a smile. Her eyes seemed to be nothing but pupils. They shone in her face like dark buttons. She looked so funny and friendly that Rosie couldn't help smiling back. She only came up to Rosie's shoulder and seemed to be so fat and round that Rosie almost expected her to bounce rather than walk. She took Rosie's arm and squeezed it.

'You know, my dear, I think if we stay here much longer we're going to drown standing up.' She giggled. 'Come inside, warm yourself at the fire and have something hot to eat. Then you can tell us the whole story from beginning to end. What do you think of that, eh?'

Rosie was too out of breath to speak. The rain dripped from her hair; from the end of her nose. It would be lovely to sit in front of a warm fire. 'Yes please,' she said.

'That's settled, then, and after we can decide what's best to do about Thingummy and all these people you've lost. Come along.'

She tucked her arm beneath Rosie's and led her to the door of the rambling old house that was almost invisible behind a curtain of ivy. They stood in the porch. It was full of sacks, spades, trowels, bulbs, and gardening boots. The old woman sat down on a wooden wall seat and grunting loudly began to tug at her boots.

68

'I don't want to be a nuisance,' Rosie said.

'Nuisance! Nonsense. Don't think about it, my dear. Sybilla and I so rarely see anyone. It's quite a treat for us to have some company. Especially children. Makes us feel quite young again.' And she giggled, her eyes almost disappearing into a web of creases.

'Thank you,' said Rosie.

The woman sat down on the floor and extended her short plump legs. 'Give us a heave ho with me booties,' she said.

Rosie tugged them off.

The old woman blew her nose loudly and giggled once more. 'Now, what's your name, child?' Rosie told her.

'That's nice. And you must call me Mouldy.'

'Mouldy?'

'I know, it's a silly old name, isn't it. My real name's Grimoulde but Sybilla called me Mouldy when I was little. It was a joke really.' She stood up, her arms out. 'And now I look like a round old bun that's gone off a bit, don't I? So Mouldy it is.'

She opened the heavy front door and Rosie followed her into a dark passage. 'Goodness, it's dark in here. Can't have that, ɔan we?' She bent down and lit two paraffin lamps. 'Lucky you found us really,' she said. 'There are some strange people hereabouts.'

The flaring lamp washed her pouched and wrinkled face in gold and pink. The passage smelt of paraffin. Mouldy blew out the match and held up the lamp.

'Just see if she's in,' she whispered and winked at Rosie. 'Sybilla,' she called. 'Sybilla.'

There was no answer.

Mouldy coughed apologetically. 'It's my sister,' she whispered confidentially. 'She's a bit hard of hearing too. I'll tell her you're here. She gets nervous of strange company.'

'Oh, I'm sorry, I don't want to worry her,' said Rosie. She moved towards the door.

Mouldy stopped her. 'Don't be silly. Wouldn't dream of letting you go out into that wicked world alone at this time of night.'

A thin, imperious voice rang down the corridor. 'Grimoulde? Grimoulde, is that you?'

Mouldy stiffened. The smile disappeared from her face. She hung her shawl on the back of the door. 'Oh dear,' she whispered, 'she called me Grimoulde. That's always a bad sign. When she's in a good mood she calls me Mouldy.' She sang out, 'Only me, dear. I've got a visitor.'

She wrinkled her nose amiably. 'You wait here, dear. I'll tell her who you are; put her mind at rest, you see.' She took Rosie's arm and squeezed it. 'Now, don't let her frighten you,' she whispered confidentially. 'Bark's worse than her bite. Won't be a ticky-boo.'

She picked up one of the lamps and shuffled down the corridor, her long brown skirt trailing on the dusty flagstones. She turned and winked at Rosie before disappearing through a curtained door.

Rosie looked about her. She gasped and drew back in horror. From the wall an inch from her face a sharp-nosed, furry creature snarled at her, his pointed teeth bared. Slowly she uncovered her face. The creature hadn't moved. He stared at her with a cold and glassy stare. Rosie realized with a sigh of relief that the stoat was stuffed and perched on a small shelf. She took the paraffin lamp from the hook on the wall and held it aloft. The walls were covered with stuffed animals, some in glass cases. Here a snarling wild cat struggled to free itself from a snake that wound its length about the cat's throat and body. The snake's jaws gaped as though its fangs were about to bite. On the opposite wall, encased in glass, a ferret carried a rat away in its teeth through mossy undergrowth. Everywhere the skulls of long-dead creatures peered down at her. From the ceiling hung bats and birds, their wings tied to the ceiling as though they were in flight. Their shadows danced in the lamplight. The eyes of the dead creatures seemed to glare at her. She shuddered.

A door creaked open. Mouldy's smiling face appeared. She beckoned. 'Psst, Rosie,' she whispered, 'it's all right. She'd like to see you.'

Rosie replaced the lamp and walked down the corridor. Mouldy held open a tattered curtain and pushed open the door. Rosie entered a dark, low-ceilinged room. A dull fire glowed in the grate, throwing shadows on to the ceiling. Dusty curtains hung crookedly from the tiny windows and there was a sickly sweet smell of incense. From the beams hung long spiders' webs, black and clotted with flies.

70

In the centre was a large wooden table piled with greasy bowls and spoons. Three thin black cats crouched on the table licking the bowls. The largest of them leapt nimbly and soundlessly from the table and crossed to the fire on which a large iron pot bubbled. He stood on his hind legs and rested both paws on the rim of the pot and began to sniff at the contents.

From the darkness at the other end of the room came a cry and a silver-topped cane clattered across the floor striking the cat. He uttered a wail of dismay, skittered between Rosie's legs and leapt on to a large easy chair where he began to wash himself disdainfully. The other two cats watched with interest and then resumed their meal. Rosie gazed through the gloom in the direction from which the stick had been flung. She saw a shadowy figure.

'Light another lamp, Grimoulde. Let the child see me.'

Mouldy struck a match. Rosie could see her hand trembling. She dropped the match.

'Give it to me, you stupid old baggage. You'll send us all up in flames.'

A match scratched once more and sputtered into flame. The wick caught and the paraffin lamp flared, throwing tongues of light and shadow across the walls and ceilings. A tall, dark handsome woman sat upright in a chair. Her hair was jet black and scraped back so tightly from her forehead that it seemed to pull her whole face back. Her eyes glittered. On her lap sat a beady-eyed raven whose glossy black head she stroked with a gloved hand. The raven played with a rag of material, pulling at it with his great beak.

The lady stared at Rosie, not speaking. Rosie shuffled her feet. She was aware of the water dripping on to the dusty floor from her clothes. She felt like a rabbit who was being inspected by a snake.

Finally the woman spoke. Her voice was soft, almost a whisper.

'Take the lamp, Mouldy.'

Mouldy placed the lamp on the table. The cats reared back for an instant and then resumed their evening meal.

'Is this the child?'

Mouldy shuffled forward rubbing her hands together nervously. 'Yes, Sybilla dear.'

71

'My sight is dim, my dear. You must forgive an old lady.'

She took the raven, holding both his legs above the claws and placed him on the back of her ornately carved chair. She held out her hand. 'My cane, Grimoulde.'

Mouldy picked up the silver-topped cane and handed it to her. Like a queen she descended towards them, her stiff black gown whispering across the dusty floor. She stared into Rosie's face as though it were a book she was intent on reading. She smiled. 'A pretty child, Mouldy. Very pretty. Tell me, my dear, where did you spring from?'

'I told you, Sybilla, I was sitting on the bench after picking some spuds like you asked me when . . . ' Mouldy began.

A thump from the cane silenced her. The raven turned his glossy head and croaked; plucked at the feathers on his breast.

'Who asked you to speak?'

Mouldy bowed her head. 'Nobody, Sybilla.'

'Mmm.' She turned to Rosie. 'Grimoulde is a kindly person but sometimes her tongue runs away with her. I've told her many times that if it continues to wag we shall have to do something about it. Shall we not, Grimoulde?'

'Yes, sister.'

The tall lady uttered a dismissive snort. 'Ha!' She turned her glossy head sideways but her eyes remained fixed on Rosie. 'Did you hear that, dear child? Did you hear what she called me, mmm?'

Rosie didn't know whether she was expected to answer or not. She shifted her feet. 'I . . . er . . . '

Sybilla's voice cut across her. 'Sister! She calls me sister. Sister!' Her voice cut shrilly through the room. The cats stopped their licking and turned their heads. The raven flapped his wings. Sybilla smiled, her voice soft once more. 'And I out of the kindness of my heart permit it. But there is no blood between us.' She smiled. 'No blood at all. Mouldy's a foundling. A poor lost slum child. We took her in. Isn't that so, Mouldy?'

'Yes,' said Mouldy. 'And you know that I'm eternally grateful for it, Sybilla.'

Sybilla nodded. She began to walk in a small circle about Rosie, her head flung back, inspecting her closely. 'Quite so. You see Grimoulde has been with us for so long that she sometimes gets above herself. We allow her to call us sister now and then which makes her think she's as good as we. But of course she isn't. Not by a very long chalk. Are you, Grimoulde?'

Mouldy looked at the floor. 'No, Sybilla.'

'You would do well to remember that.'

She stopped in front of Rosie. She smiled but her eyes glittered. 'Well, my dear, how extremely clever of you to find us and how fortunate for us. Two poor, lonely old ladies. We have so little young company, you see.'

She offered Rosie her cheek, closing her eyes. 'You may,' she said.

'Pardon?' said Rosie.

'Kiss me, child. Kiss me.'

Hesitantly Rosie leaned forward and touched her lips to the proffered cheek. The skin was parchment-thin and cold to the touch. She wanted to wipe her mouth but thought it might appear rude.

Sybilla stared into Rosie's eyes. 'Old skin,' she muttered sadly. 'An old woman's wrinkled skin. Once I had skin like yours, my dear.'

She removed her right glove. Her fingers were long and thin, almost transparent. But it was the nails that astonished Rosie. They were immensely long. So long that they curled and corkscrewed back on themselves.

'Such beautiful young skin.' She caressed Rosie's cheek. She felt the thin hard edge of the nails scratch her face.

'Skin like yours, my dear. Smooth as a rose petal. What is your name, child?'

'Rosie.'

'Rosie,' whispered Sybilla closing her eyes and replacing the glove. 'Of course, Rosie.' She rolled the name on her tongue as though she were tasting it. She smiled. 'How well it suits you. Skin like a rose and so full of young life.'

Rosie tried to smile. Sybilla put her lips to Rosie's ear. 'And you must call me Sybilla,' she whispered. She sounded it out clearly and slowly. 'Sy-bi-lla.'

'Sybilla,' repeated Rosie.

'Perfect.' She smiled a thin-lipped smile and her gaze flickered over Rosie's face. She returned to her chair and patted the seat

73

beside her. 'Come, you must tell me all about . . . Oh, what was his name?'

'Alastair,' said Rosie.

'Alastair, of course. And Grimoulde tells me he had an unfortunate accident.'

Rosie told her about Alastair hurting his ankle and of her journey to the river and how she had returned and found that Alastair had disappeared. Of the diary, the pit, and her memory loss she said nothing.

'Disappeared? What do you think of that, Grimoulde? Disappeared. This sounds an utter mystery.' She leaned her head towards Rosie. 'Do tell.'

So Rosie told her about Alastair and the pit and the boat. Sybilla listened intently her eyes never leaving Rosie's and then she leaned forward smiling. 'And are Alastair and Rosie old chums?'

Rosie was hesitant about telling of her memory loss. She stopped in mid sentence.

Sybilla glanced at her.

'The story has ceased. What is it, child? Don't you trust us?' Her black eyes stared into Rosie's.

'I . . . ' began Rosie.

'You don't wish to tell me more, is that it?'

'No, it's just that I . . . I . . . ' she stuttered.

'And quite right, dear child. What business is it of ours? None at all. If you have a secret then that is what it must remain. Locked up in your heart and the key thrown away.' She took Rosie's hands in both of hers; stared deeply into her eyes. Her voice was a whisper. 'For the heart of a child is the most secret place in the world. When you wish to tell us anything, wish for a shoulder to cry on or for an ear to pour your troubles into, I'll be only too happy to listen and to give what advice I can. Grimoulde and I are famous for our shoulders and our ears. Are we not, Grimoulde? Grimoulde!'

'Oh yes, Sybilla.'

'Yes.' Sybilla stroked Rosie's arm. She frowned. 'But, my dear, how thoughtless of us. This garment is quite drenched. You must change at once or you'll catch your death and that would never do.'

Rosie protested, 'Oh no, I couldn't. I . . . '

Sybilla waved her excuses away.

'Off with those damp things.'

From about her neck she took a dirty piece of string on which were three brass keys.

'Grimoulde, be so kind as to bring dry clothes and a towel for the dear girl.'

Grimoulde hurried from the room closing the door softly behind her.

Sybilla held Rosie's hand. She squeezed it. 'And your poor little friend Alastair out in the wild wood on such a night. Not even a dog should be out in this weather. Not even a dog.' She looked about her as though someone might be listening. 'And this Alastair, are you fond of him? Of course you are, I can see it in your eyes. Now, tell Sybilla, how did you come to lose each other?'

And in the face of those unblinking dark eyes Rosie told her about her diary and the pit and how she thought it had been dug on purpose.

When she heard this Sybilla frowned. 'On purpose! What, to trap children? Fie, Rosie. Nobody could be so wicked.' She glanced at the door and then back to Rosie. 'Listen to me, Rosie. Tomorrow, you and I will look for him and . . . '

The door opened and Mouldy hurried in, smiling. In her arms she carried a towel and a heap of clothing. Sybilla placed her finger on her lips. 'We'll say no more about it, child,' she whispered. 'It can be our secret, Rosie. You like secrets, don't you? All children do. And so do I.' Her mouth smiled but her eyes did not. She glanced up at the waiting Grimoulde. 'Grimoulde, my darling, Rosie and I have been having such an interesting chat, haven't we, Rosie? But we can't tell Grimoulde what about because it was a secret, you see.'

She took a full length pale coloured dress decorated with blue daisies from Mouldy and held it up in front of Rosie. She cocked her head on one side and eyed her. 'This should fit perfectly. Off with that.' And she began to pull the jumper over Rosie's head. Rosie drew back.

Sybilla glanced at her sister. 'The child is modest. And quite right too. We must leave her to dress in peace, Grimoulde. We shall leave her. Come along.' She ushered her sister away. At the

75

door she turned. 'Rosie dear, we shall prepare a bed. When you're ready let us know,' she whispered. She smiled and went out, closing the door behind her.

Rosie looked about her at the shadowed room. The raven was watching her. Rosie moved hesitantly forward. On a rush of wings, the raven swooped across the room. Rosie ducked, holding both hands to her head. The raven flapped past and then back at her screeching hoarsely. He landed on the table sending the remaining cats leaping fearfully for safety. For an instant he stared at Rosie, his head cocked, then he began to tear at the remains of the food, his claws scratching and shuffling on the wooden table.

Rosie crept forward towards the dress and the towel. The raven stopped eating. He swivelled his glossy head and fixed his black eyes on her. A step at a time Rosie advanced, her eyes on the raven. She leaned forward and picked up the towel and the garment. He followed her with his eyes. She walked backwards a step at a time till her back was to the wall. The bird seemed to lose interest in her and resumed eating. She heard meat tearing between his claws and his beak.

She stood by the fire and slowly removed her clothes. She felt uncomfortable undressing in front of the bird.

Only a bird, silly, she thought. Nothing to be afraid of.

And yet she was afraid. She had visions of herself pulling the jumper over her head and the raven attacking her. Beating his wings and scrabbling at her face. As quickly as she could she tried to pull the jumper and the blouse off at the same time. Too quickly. What she had dreaded happened. The arms were inside out. They twined about her neck. The blouse tightened about her head. She could see nothing. She searched feverishly for the buttons of her blouse. She yanked savagely at the jumper. It wouldn't move.

'Get off, get off.' She couldn't breathe. With a final jerk, bursting the buttons, she freed herself. Her face was hot and rough. She turned her back on the bird who was still busily engaged in eating and drew off her jeans. She dried herself on the towel. Her heart beat rapidly.

Why am I so nervous? she wondered. They've been very kind. But that dark one frightens me. The way she looks at you. It's as though she looks into your soul. And those fingernails give me the shivers.

She turned. The raven was watching her with his beady eyes, his head cocked as though he were listening. He blinked and would not look away. Rosie turned her back and pulled the dress hurriedly over her head and shoulders and smoothed the material down. It was dry and smelt of must as though it had lain forgotten for many years at the bottom of a drawer. The fire spluttered and crackled. She folded her clothes before it.

Should she tell the sisters that she was ready?

Something rubbed at her legs. It was the cat. She bent and picked him up but in a sudden explosion of movement he leapt up on to her shoulder, sinking his claws in. Rosie gasped with pain and brushed the cat roughly from her. He sprang for the chair and then the table where the bird spread his wings and pecked at him. The cat leaped to the floor spitting at the bird.

Hunger ate at Rosie. They had promised something to eat. It was wrong of her to think so badly of them. Old people were often eccentric. They'd given her warmth and shelter. She felt ashamed of herself for being so ungrateful. When they came in she would tell them how thankful she was. She tiptoed to the door and put her ear to it. A floorboard creaked. She heard the sound of whispering.

She was about to call out when she saw something lying on the floor. It was the torn rag the bird had picked at. Where had she seen it before? She bent down and picked it up. Despite the claw marks and the holes she could see that it wasn't a rag but the remains of a scarf. In one corner was written the letter 'A'. The scarf she had given to Alastair. An involuntary cry escaped her. She staggered backwards. Her head swam.

In her mind's eye she saw Sybilla's glittering eye. Her lips whispering. *Your poor little friend Alastair out in the wild wood . . . Not even a dog should be out in this weather . . . Rosie, you and I will look for him.* Lies. It had all been lies. Alastair was here somewhere. In this house. Unless . . .

She remembered the black carriage, the black stallion, the dark bird that had attacked Ned by the river, the pit, the diary. Sybilla. *Her! It had all been her!* Her head swam. She thought she was going to faint. She held the scarf up with both hands. Buried her face in it. A hoarse scream. The scarf was torn from her. She fell back against the wall covering her face with her hands. The raven sat on his perch contemplating her, his black beak picking at the scarf.

11

One thought pounded in Rosie's brain. This was a dangerous place. She had to get away. She ran to the windows at the back of the room and flung back the moth-eaten curtains. Shutters! Wooden shutters. She pulled at them desperately. They squeaked and rattled but were fast. Sybilla would be back soon.

She put her ear to the door. A dress rustled along the passageway. A voice whispered. Further off she heard faint laughter. Then a door creaked open and there was a rush of wind. The door closed, echoing through the house. Rosie closed her eyes and put her back to the door. The raven watched her, his beak open. Footsteps climbed the stairs. Silence.

Slowly she turned the knob and stepped into the corridor. Empty. She heard footsteps upstairs and crouched back into the shadows. She glanced upwards. A black skirt billowed through the banister rails. She glanced up the corridor. How far was it to the front door? Ten paces? Twelve at the most. She took a deep breath and tiptoed past the stuffed, wild creatures whose eyes glittered at her from the walls. Upstairs a door closed. She waited an instant and then put her hand on the latch. Lifted it and pulled. It wouldn't move. Gritting her teeth she pulled harder. It was locked.

'Grimoulde!'

Sybilla's voice rang out. Rosie drew back, crushing herself against the wall. Her ears sang with blood. She heard Grimoulde answer though she couldn't make out the words. She heard the legs of a bed scraping across wooden floorboards. Somebody laughed. Rosie took a deep breath. There must be another way out; a back door somewhere. There was always a back door. Wasn't there? Perhaps down the passage.

She ran on tiptoe past the foot of the wooden stairs and the room from which she had just emerged. It was darker now. No lamps lit the gloom. She crept slowly until her hands encountered a door. To her relief it swung open to her touch. She slipped through. She felt before her with her foot. There was nothing. Emptiness. She lowered her foot and struck stone. A step. Then another and another. The passage continued.

Holding her hands before her she advanced blindly. What was that beneath her foot? Something small and hard. Perhaps a key. She heard footsteps on the landing. She knelt down, her hands sweeping the floor. Her fingers closed on something cold, metallic, and heavy. She picked it up and felt the weight of it in her hand. Her forefinger traced the relief pattern. Even in the dark she knew what it was. The cross. Alastair's medal! He was here somewhere.

She hung it by the ribbon about her neck and pulled herself upright. Took another step into the darkness. Her foot caught something. It clattered to the floor. The sound was terrible. She cursed her clumsiness. Listening, she crouched in the dark. Her hand found a broom. She lodged it against the wall. She stood once more. Moved forward into the darkness.

Her fumbling hand encountered a panel of wood. A door. Her hopes rose. He was here somewhere. She was sure of it. Somewhere behind the door. Somewhere close. Her hands searched the door seeking for the handle. Why wasn't there any light? She touched cold metal. She tugged at the door knob. An involuntary gasp of despair escaped from her. This door too was locked fast. She put her face to the door. Called softly. 'Alastair. Are you there? Alastair, it's me, Rosie.'

Was that a voice she heard? Faint and distant like a voice in a dream. Or was it her imagination? She couldn't be certain.

She heard footsteps. Sybilla's voice. The creak of the stairs. They were coming back. She whispered through the door as much for her own sake as for Alastair's.

'Alastair, if you're there, I have to go. But I'll be back. Somehow. I won't leave you.'

She had to reach the room before them. She would play for time. Be innocent. Pretend she suspected nothing. She had to get back before them. She turned and hurried back towards the room. Reached the door. Pushed it open. Crept through. Now there was light. She heard Sybilla's voice descending the stairs. Now she was at the living room door. She was about to enter.

'Rosie!'

Sybilla stood at the foot of the stairs. She played with the keys idly. Grimoulde peered over her shoulder. Rosie turned. She felt her heart pounding.

'How did you find it?' asked Sybilla.

Rosie stuttered. 'Find?' She felt herself blushing. Her voice was thick. 'Find it?'

'Yes, my dear. How did you find it? The dress?'

'Oh, the dress.'

'Yes, of course. What did you think I meant?'

'N . . . nothing,' stuttered Rosie.

Sybilla smiled. 'Well?'

Rosie laughed nervously. 'The dress.' She plucked at the skirt. Smiled what she hoped was an innocent smile. 'Oh . . . er . . . yes, it fits very well. It's lovely. Thank you.'

'You hear that, Grimoulde. Fits well. I knew it would.'

Sybilla looked at her in silence. Her eyes glanced up the dark corridor. Her voice had an edge of mockery. 'Rosie dear, were you thinking of going somewhere?'

'Going?' Rosie realized she was standing in the open door. 'Oh no. I was dressed, you see, and . . . er . . . wondered where you were. I came to show you the . . . er . . . dress.'

Sybilla sighed sympathetically. 'To show us the dress. We're neglecting you, my dear. We were just preparing a bed.'

'Ah, I see. Thank you.'

'Think nothing of it, dear child.'

She swept forward, her arm about Rosie, and led her back into the room.

'Turn about.'

'Turn?'

'Yes. Let us see the dress.'

'Oh!'

Rosie held up the hem and twirled in a circle. They both watched her, smiling. Sybilla clapped her hands. 'It's charming,' she murmured. 'Why, it might have been made for you, my dear.' She took Rosie's hand and led her to the table. 'Come, my dear, you must be starving. We must eat.'

With her cane she brushed the protesting raven from the table. He fluttered protesting on to the back of the carved chair. The remnants of the scarf fell from his beak to the floor. Had

81

Sybilla seen it? Recognized what it was? Rosie walked forward intending to sweep it out of sight under the table.

'Rosie!'

'Yes?'

'You will sit here,' said Sybilla indicating the chair at the head of the table. Sybilla's foot brushed the scarf. How was it possible she had not noticed it?

'Thank you,' said Rosie. She pretended to stumble and placed her foot over the scarf.

'Are you all right?'

'Oh yes,' said Rosie, 'just clumsy.' As she sat down she swept the scarf under the table. The raven watched her curiously.

Mouldy placed the tureen of broth on the table and wiped the dirty bowls on her skirt. Sybilla leaned over the tureen and inhaled deeply. An expression of ecstasy crossed her face. She closed her eyes.

'Heavenly aroma,' she whispered.

Grimoulde ladled the grey liquid into the bowls. The two sisters began to eat noisily. Rosie stared at the soup in her bowl. Soft white lumps floated in its greyness and a cracked skin extended over the surface.

Sybilla glanced at her. 'Come, eat up, my dear. We don't stand on ceremony here.'

Rosie reluctantly picked up her spoon. The sight of the broth and its rank smell drove out her hunger. She sank her spoon into the soup, breaking the skin. Slowly she raised it to her mouth. A large piece of fat floated in her spoon. They watched her expectantly. She smiled and felt the soft lump fill her mouth. She found it impossible to swallow. A jagged edge of splintered bone scratched the roof of her mouth. She covered her mouth with her hand and surreptitiously slid the fat and gristle on to the floor. The cats gathered about her feet purring and spitting. Sybilla looked at her enquiringly.

Rosie managed another smile. 'Very nice,' she croaked. Sybilla returned the smile and continued eating. Every opportunity she had Rosie slipped another indigestible lump beneath the table. The cats rubbed at her legs. Finally she put her spoon down, wiping her lips, and gave a sigh of what she hoped sounded like satisfaction. Sybilla and Grimoulde looked at her enquiringly.

Sybilla frowned at the soup that remained in Rosie's bowl. She clicked her tongue.

'Is that all you are going to eat, my dear?'

Rosie patted her stomach and blew out her cheeks. 'I'm really full up.'

'We just adore crow soup, do we not, sister?' said Sybilla.

Crow soup! Rosie swallowed. She noticed a small black feather floating on the surface.

'Won't you try a little more. Just to please. You did like it, didn't you?'

'Oh yes,' said Rosie, 'it was lovely.'

Sybilla smiled and ladled another spoonful into her bowl. 'Well?'

Reluctantly Rosie picked up her spoon once more. She sank it into the bowl and raised the grey, lukewarm contents to her lips. She swallowed. The thick liquid refused to go down. She coughed. Then swallowed harder. She thought she would be sick and put her hand over her mouth. She retched and managed to disguise it with a cough. She gulped and felt the unwholesome brew trickling down her throat. She closed her eyes with revulsion. Her eyes were watering. She put her spoon down.

'No more?' Sybilla enquired.

'No thank you,' Rosie said. 'I think I must be too sleepy to eat any more.'

Sybilla slapped her hand to her forehead.

'The poor child. How thoughtless! Look at the time. There she is dead with sleep and we keeping her up. Bed for you, dear child.'

Sybilla picked the keys from the table and looped the string about her throat. She rose from the table and Rosie followed her to the door.

As they climbed the stairs Sybilla said, 'We have two bedrooms but I thought you might like to share with us.'

'Share?'

'But if you like there is a spare room. But you might be lonely.'

Rosie said quickly, 'Oh, I'd rather have a room to myself.'

'Well, we shall be disappointed, shall we not, Grimoulde?'

'Very disappointed,' said Grimoulde who was bringing up the rear.

Rosie invented rapidly. Her head buzzed.

'You see, I'm an only child. I always sleep alone. I'm used to it.'

'Just as you like, my dear.'

They reached a square landing at the top of the stairs. Sybilla nodded to a door on her right. 'That is our bedroom, Rosie dear.' She opened a door on her left and stood back for Rosie to enter. 'This is where you will sleep.'

She smiled and gestured with her hand.

Hesitantly Rosie stepped forward and entered the bedroom.

12

Rosie looked round the musty bedroom. It smelt of mouldering clothes, paraffin, and mice. Dust hovered in the flickering lamplight. Against the wall furthest from the door stood a fourposter bed, one leg supported by three large books. Sybilla swept back the musty heavy drapes that hung gapingly about the bed. A large moth fluttered out of the fabric and beat frenziedly at the lamp. She heard the sizzle as it incinerated.

Sybilla turned over the sheets. 'A bed fit for a queen,' she said. Her dark eyes gleamed in the lamplight.

'We'll leave you the lamp to undress by, Rosie dear,' she said setting the light down on a small wooden table in the centre of the room. She turned at the door. 'When you're ready we'll tuck you in.'

They left the room. Rosie could hear them whispering.

She crept to the door and closed it. She pressed her hand on the bed. The mattress was hard and lumpy. Dust covered her finger tips. A nightdress lay folded on the pillow. Was she expected to wear it? She picked it up gingerly as though it might contain a sleeping toad or snake. It was of thick flannel, pock-marked with moth holes, and smelt faintly of sweat. The thought of it touching her flesh filled Rosie with revulsion. A large spider scuttled from beneath the folds and on to the floor then disappeared beneath the bed. Rosie sat on its edge. It sagged visibly. She stared about her.

A mouse emerged from beneath the bed and sat on its haunches washing its face with its front paws. The thought of it climbing up on to the bed, its tiny feet scampering across her arm and face made Rosie grimace. She took off her shoe and hurled it at the tiny creature. It scuttled from sight beneath the bed.

Rosie climbed up on to the bed holding up the nightdress. She mustn't give Sybilla any grounds for suspicion. She would be obedient and polite and grateful. She decided to wear the nightdress. She slipped it on over the dress she was wearing. Then, clothed apart from her shoes, she slipped between the cold sheets and pulled the curtains about her.

It was like lying in a small room. She lay there staring at the ceiling shivering slightly, listening to the scampering and scratching mice above her head. The wind gusted in the eaves and rain was falling steadily on the roof. A shutter banged persistently.

Was there a window? she wondered. Might it be open? Better look now before they returned. While she still had the lamp. Quietly she pulled back the covers and put her left leg out of the bed.

Sybilla stood there the lamp held aloft.

'If there's anything you need,' she said, 'don't hesitate to call.'

Rosie sank back pulling the coverlet up to her chin. She remembered her promise. She managed a smile. 'Thank you. You're very kind.'

'You're a dear,' said Sybilla. She pulled back the curtains and gazed down on her. Her face flickered. She bent down. 'Now, give Sybilla a goodnight kiss.' Rosie felt the cold lips on her cheek.

She knew Sybilla was expecting a kiss in return. She loathed the idea. But she had to. 'Thank you,' she whispered and touched the thin cheek with her lips. She smelt of camphor. Rosie tried to keep back the shiver that shook her frame. But she couldn't help herself. Her body convulsed in revulsion.

'Not cold are we, Rosie dear?' Sybilla cooed.

Rosie managed another smile. 'Just a little.'

'Then we must tuck her in, mustn't we, Grimoulde?'

And the two of them pulled the sheets taut as drum skins and tucked them in hard. Rosie's arms were pinioned to her sides. It was as though she were tightly bandaged down.

They stood side by side looking down at her. 'Goodnight, Rosie dear.' At the door Sybilla gave a little wave. 'We'll take the lamp.' She pointed across the hall. 'Don't forget I'm only a step away.'

The door closed softly behind them.

Rosie was alone. She lay for she knew not how long, staring wide-eyed into the thick dark. She heard whispers and the creak of floorboards from across the landing.

She felt immensely tired. But she knew she mustn't sleep. Eyes

86

open, her body rigid, she began to repeat over and over again in a hoarse whisper, 'Don't sleep, don't sleep.'

But the repeated sound of her own voice only made her drowsy and she jerked suddenly into wakefulness. She sat up and tried to think of a plan. Her mind wandered to Alastair. He was somewhere in the house. She wondered if he was thinking of her. She'd heard of people doing such things. You concentrated so hard that the other person knew what you were thinking. Like a mental radio. She closed her eyes hard.

Alastair. Are you there somewhere? It's me, Rosie. I'm thinking about you. I'm here in the house. I miss you. It'll be all right. Really it will.

The message was more confident than she felt. Perhaps Alastair was thinking of her. It was no good if they were both thinking at the same time. The messages might collide in mid air. She tried to make her mind blank. Her eyelids drooped. In her dream she was running along the edge of a high cliff. A girl in white stood staring out; the sea wind blew her long white skirt.

'It's better in this picture,' the girl said smiling and took her hand. Rosie looked down at the wrinkled sea far below them.

'Don't worry,' said the girl, 'I can fly. It's easy. Better than being in this place neither dead nor alive. Trust me.' Then taking a deep breath she launched herself, arms spread out, from the high cliff and Rosie felt herself falling.

'Hold still!'

At the sound of the voice she woke instantly. Sybilla! Sybilla was in the room.

'Hold the lamp still, I say.'

Rosie lay rigid. She watched the light and shadows dance. They were approaching the bed. Coming towards her. She closed her eyes. Breathed as evenly as she could pretending to sleep. She heard the curtains move; sensed the bloom of light through her shut lids. They were leaning over her. Staring. She felt Sybilla's breath on her cheek. Her body seemed to itch all over. She longed to move. To scratch. To blink her eyes. A cough began to tickle at the back of her throat. She longed to swallow. But daren't.

'Asleep.'

'You think so?'

87

'Of course, Sybilla.'

'Pretty thing.'

'You're not going to do it now?'

'No. Morning will do.'

'Seems a shame, Sybilla.'

'Shame!' Sybilla's voice cut through the darkness like a whiplash.

'I mean her being so pretty and all.'

'Ha! You're a sentimental fool.'

'I wonder if she's dreaming?'

'If she is it will be her last.'

'Sybilla, what if she wakes and tries to escape?'

'You'll be there.'

'What should I do?'

'What should you do? Why, kill her, of course. Kill her quick.'

She heard the curtain swish shut. Heard the door shut softly and the light disappear.

She sat up shaking. *Kill her, of course.*

A moan broke from her. She ran her shaking hands through her hair. She had to get away. Had to. No use waiting till morning. Now. Now. No time to lose. The dark was like a black bandage winding about her. She fumbled for her shoes. Something scampered on tiny feet across the floor. She felt her way along the wall then to the door carrying her shoes in her hand. Softly with gritted teeth she opened it an inch or two. Across the landing, beneath the door opposite, a crack of light showed. She shut the door quickly.

She couldn't stop shaking. *Kill her.* She found difficulty breathing. It was as though she was drowning; drowning in air. The walls and the floor began to sway. She almost fell. She had to have air. Clinging hard to the wall she felt her way to the window. She had expected the shutters to be locked but they opened easily. She fumbled for the window catch and her hand closed on iron bars. It was a prison. She turned away clenching her fists. *Why, kill her, of course.*

She shook her head. The keys, she must get the keys. In her mind's eye she saw them strung about Sybilla's scrawny throat. How could she take them without waking her? How? The very thought of it made her shudder. She stood stiffly in the corner of the strange, dark bedroom, her hands rigid to her sides. She would have to wait. That was it. Wait, wait until Sybilla was asleep. Then take the keys. Untie the knot as she slept and steal out. She saw herself doing it. Advancing on tiptoe across the bedroom floor. Standing over the sleeping form. She saw her trembling hand stretching down to the throat. Taking the string. Lifting it. Slowly, so slowly, untying the knot. Nearly, nearly. *Noooooooooo!* Sybilla jerked suddenly upright, eyes wild, teeth bared, hissing.

Rosie shook the vision away. Oh God, I can't, she whimpered to herself. I can't do it.

But she had to. Had to. There was no other way. How long should she wait? There was no clock. No moon. No light. Half an hour? Would that be time enough? What was half an hour? Sixty seconds in a minute. Sixty minutes in an hour. Divide by two. One thousand eight hundred. Call it two thousand. She began to count. One and two and three and . . . At a hundred her head jerked back. She had almost fallen asleep; fallen asleep standing up.

She pinched herself until the pain made her gasp. She started from the beginning, counting once more. At two thousand she counted another fifty just to be on the safe side. But really she was doing it out of fear. Fear of Sybilla lying in the next room. Sybilla with the coal black eyes, the corkscrew nails, and the cruel heart. Sybilla who leaned over her and whispered *Kill her quick*. What if somehow she knew what Rosie was thinking? Lying there, her eyes open. Listening to her thoughts. Smiling. Waiting.

It was time. There was no putting it off any longer. She had to do it. Now. She hid her face in her hands and gave a dry, convulsive sob. If she didn't do it now. She never would.

She crept to the door and opened it slowly. She blessed it for not creaking. Across the landing to that other door was eight steps. She was there. She stood for a moment. She could hear herself breathing; hear her heart pounding. She breathed deeply to calm herself. Slowly, so slowly her hand ached, she turned the door knob; pushed the door an inch at a time.

She prayed. Please God let her not wake up.

A grey light seaped through the shutters. She moved forward an inch. Then another. Her eyes grew accustomed to the gloom.

89

Sybilla's bed lay diagonally across from the door some three or four feet from the shuttered window.

And in it lay Sybilla.

Rosie crept towards the bed letting her feet fall softly as though she were walking on eggs. Her hand closed over the brass rail at the foot of the bed. She could see Sybilla's face now; shadowed and strangely beautiful but even in sleep utterly cold. She had loosened her hair and the tresses flowed across the counterpane like a black river. She wore no gloves and the long twisted nails curved out from her fingertips. She went closer. So close she could hear Sybilla's breathing. Was she really sleeping? Could it be a trap? Too late now to turn back.

She inched closer and stood between the bed and the shutter. There it was about her throat. The dirty length of string and on the end of it three keys. Rosie licked her lips. Closed her eyes an instant. Opened them. It was time. She stretched out her hand above the sleeping form; her fingers shook uncontrollably.

Don't shake, hand. Please don't shake.

She tried once more. How small the distance from her hand to that throat. And yet it seemed like a chasm. Now she was nearer; could almost touch the string. Another inch. Half an inch. Her fingers touched it. She lifted a twist of dark hair to one side. Her fingers found the knot. She needed both hands to unpick it. Trying not to breathe, her fingers moving as delicately as possible, she began to pick at the knot.

Suddenly the breathing stopped. The beringed hand on the counterpane moved. The fingers crawled like a jewelled spider scuttling across the counterpane. Sybilla uttered a deep sudden sigh and turned. Her arm moved in sleep. Lowered over Rosie's hand, trapping it. Sybilla's lips moved. In the depth of her sleep from whatever dreams Sybilla dreamed she muttered aloud *Kill her.* The thin lips smiled and then she was silent once more settling into sleep.

The keys lay on the blanket now. That was easier. But Rosie's hand was trapped. She pressed it down into the bed then with the other holding the wrist she withdrew it, as though it were something not her own, from under Sybilla's arm. She flexed her fingers and once more took hold of the knot. Gently she began to pick at it, softly at first, then harder, almost recklessly. Sybilla murmured. Rosie could see the balls of her eyes rolling beneath the shut lids.

The knot was slipping. And then suddenly it was done. Rosie drew the keys along the length of string. Felt them cold and heavy in her palm. She had them! Had them.

She turned, wanting to run but forcing herself to move slowly. Any moment she expected to hear a voice like a whiplash behind her. She was at the door. Out on the landing. A step at a time she descended the stairs and made for the back door. She listened. Nothing moved. Outside the open door where she had eaten the night before she knelt and slipped on her shoes. She thought of taking her own clothes from where they had been left before the fire. But it would all take time. And there was little time.

Down the corridor she crept blindly, her arms outstretched before her. What was that? The air beat about her as though blows rained through the air not quite striking her. Something screamed raucously in the dark. She flung up her arms beating at the thing. She felt the raven's wing slapping her face and head. He screamed again; an unending, terrible, coarse, and dead-awakening scream. No need for silence now. Down the corridor blindly Rosie rushed and through the first door. It swung shut behind her. She heard the raven clawing at the wood in fury.

And in the upstairs bedroom Sybilla awoke. Sat bolt upright. Eyes wide. Instantly awake. The girl! She lit the lamp and raced for the other room her clothes streaming behind her. Snarling she flung back the curtains from the bed. Empty! But she couldn't get far. Not without the keys. She put her hands to her throat. The keys! They were gone. A terrible, animal scream erupted from the depth of her. The girl! She had stolen the keys. Hers, Sybilla's keys. She roared with fury. She would pay for this. Teeth bared she tore down the curtains.

Below in the dark passage Rosie heard the scream and her blood turned to ice. She heard a door slamming and footsteps on the stairs. She lurched forward arms outstretched into the blackness; stumbled down three or four steps; reached out. The door! Where was the door?

Behind her, ever closer, she heard Sybilla's footsteps. Heard her voice cursing.

91

At last Rosie's fingers found the door. Fumbled the key into the lock. It wouldn't turn. Would not. She tried the second key. Why didn't they turn? It must be the third. Come on, key. Her hands were shaking uncontrollably. The keys fell to the floor. Where were they? She fell to her knees, hands scrabbling. The door behind her crashed open. In a halo of light Sybilla stood, lamp held aloft, her head thrown back, eyes staring. She laughed. Rosie's fingers closed over the keys. The awful laughter filled the passageway. Rosie scrambled to her feet. The lock! Where was the lock? Rosie prayed. Please turn. Oh, please. Sybilla's shadow fell across her, filling the passage.

She twisted her hand and suddenly the key turned freely. There was a crash. An explosion of light as the hurled lamp struck the door. The paraffin splattered and flames leapt up. Rosie heaved the door open. She removed the key. Something held her. She thought the nightdress had snagged in the door. But then realized it was Sybilla's hand clutching at her. Rosie screamed and kicked back with all her strength. But those nails, those awful corkscrew nails clung like hooks. She turned and twisted but couldn't escape. In desperation she ripped the nightdress off leaving it tattered in Sybilla's hands and pulled herself through the burning door and turned the key.

Exhausted and panting for breath she fell to her knees. She wanted to run; to get as far away from that door as she could but felt too weak to move. The door still burned but for the moment she was safe. On a hook above her head a lamp burned. Was someone else in the passage? Alastair perhaps. She stood up and unhooked the lamp. Gazed about her. There was nobody.

Then she heard it. Such a strange sound. A steady, faint, insistent scratching. It seemed to be coming from behind her. She turned. Then reeled back in horror. Through the closed door five long nails protruded. And they were moving. Squirming and wriggling like things with a life of their own. She stumbled backwards, mesmerized, unable to pull her eyes away. Then she turned and was running. Running away from that awful place. But still she heard Sybilla's screams and the faint insistent scratching. She put her hands to her ears but still she heard it. She heard it then and for many years after. Far from that place, far from that time. Deep in the deepest fathoms of her sleep she heard it. And saw it too. Saw the great door bright with leaping flames and the long nails moving. Always moving.

13

Hurriedly she walked down the narrow underground passageway holding the lamp aloft. Behind her she heard the relentless blows of an axe chopping at the door. With each blow shuddering sparks flew from it. For the moment it held. But for how long? Rosie wondered.

She quickened her pace turning the lamp this way and that peering anxiously from side to side.

'Alastair,' she called, 'Alastair.'

The cramped, chill passage seemed endless. The walls and roof were lined with the arched, dead limbs of trees but her feet splashed through puddles.

'Alastair. Alastair.'

She began to despair of finding him. Then to her left she saw a low, barred door. She held up the lamp and peered inside. At first she saw nothing but dancing shadows. Then, as she shifted the angle of the lamp the yellow light illuminated something round and yellow: a small football. She rubbed her eyes. It was no ball but a human skull and beside it the crumpled bones of a skeleton. Then another and another. She felt sick with fear and apprehension.

'Alastair.'

She moved the light again and made out a crumpled blanket abandoned on the floor. The blanket moved and a pale face emerged, a hand thrown up to ward off the light. The eyes were large and frightened. They blinked like a trapped animal's.

'Alastair!'

At the sound of the voice he backed away, terror in his eyes.

'Who . . . ?'

'It's me, Rosie.'

He limped to the door. 'Rosie!' A smile broke across his face. He reached through the bars. Their hands clasped.

'I told you I'd come back,' she said.

'And you have,' said Alastair. 'I knew you would.'

Hurriedly she put the key in the lock.

'Keep your fingers crossed.'

She uttered a silent prayer and turned the key. It grated and finally turned. She opened the door. They threw their arms about each other.

'Where is . . . ?'

Alastair couldn't bring himself to say Sybilla's name.

Rosie pointed at the blazing door. 'She set fire to it. We must be quick. She'll have it down any minute.'

They heard a searing cry and the axe strokes stopped. Smoke and flame wreathed upward setting fire to the tinder-dry branches. There was an explosion and suddenly the door burst into flames. They drew back, shielding their faces from the sudden heat.

'The whole place will go up,' shouted Alastair, his face orange in the fire's light. He clutched Rosie's hand. 'Hurry!'

His words were drowned as with a crashing roar the door pitched forward. For a second they saw a dark figure, the face convulsed with anger and hatred, orange in the light, arms raised beating savagely at the flames. Then she was gone, consumed in the leaping inferno which licked out towards them.

'It's horrible!' gasped Rosie.

'Come on,' shouted Alastair and still limping slightly led her at a run down the passage that was already beginning to blaze behind them. They turned a corner into sudden darkness.

'Where does this lead to?' Alastair panted.

'I don't know,' said Rosie peering anxiously into the small pool of light the lamp cast. 'But we can't go back. I'm hoping there'll be a back door somewhere.'

'But what if there isn't?'

'Don't say that. There has to be.'

She sounded more confident than she felt.

Suddenly Alastair stopped.

'Listen!'

'What?'

'Ssh, listen. Hear?'

'What is it?'

'Sounds like a sort of whistling.'

'A thrush. A thrush singing.'

'That means . . . '

'Yes. Come on.'

Joyful and laughing now they ran on. The voice of the thrush became louder. Alastair pointed. 'Look there!'

A fingernail of grey light appeared.

'There it is,' shouted Rosie, beginning to run. 'Told you there would be a back door.'

She couldn't help looking behind her. Light bloomed at the corner they had just rounded.

'It's the branches. The fire's catching up.'

'We'll make it.'

Alastair ran ahead. When she caught up she found him on his knees. His hands clutched a barred door not much wider than his shoulders. She knelt beside him. Beyond the bars five narrow steps dug from the earth climbed steeply to a halo of light.

'Look,' whispered Alastair.

Peering upwards she saw sunlight dappling the forest. The trees alive and heavy with leaf.

'The forest,' said Alastair, 'it comes out in the forest.'

He shook the bars. 'And we can't get out.'

'Wait. There's a lock.'

She fumbled through the keys. 'Haven't used this one yet.'

She thrust the key into the lock.

'Quick!' screamed Alastair glancing back. Smoke filled the passageway at their backs.

Desperately she turned the key.

'It won't turn,' she sobbed. 'It won't turn.'

He took the keys from her. 'Let me try.'

He pushed her to one side taking the key from her and thrust it into the lock. But it refused to turn. Rosie could feel the heat of the approaching fire now. Alastair was shouting at the key, struggling to turn it with both hands. Then in a sudden rush of temper he withdrew it and hurled it from him down the flickering passageway.

Rosie couldn't believe it. 'You stupid idiot. What did you do that for?'

'It's the wrong key. The wrong key. Why did you get the wrong key?'

'Me!' They crouched face to face screaming at one another.

'How did I know? I hate you. I hate you.' She flung herself at him throwing wild blows at his head screaming with anger. 'Now we'll never get out. And it's your stupid fault. If it hadn't been for me you'd have ended up a skeleton like all the rest.'

Sobbing she beat at him with her fists. Then just as suddenly stopped. What were they fighting for? She flung herself from him and seized the bars and shook them. How she loathed those bars. Moss climbed the trunk of a gnarled tree. Grass thrust brilliant spikes from it. How brilliantly, beautifully alive everything was. She stretched out her hand and plucked a blade of the grass and drew it back through the bars. Somewhere a blackbird was whistling.

And I'm here, she thought. And I'm going to die. She began to sob. 'I'm going to die.' It didn't seem so terrible. She was tired. So very tired.

Alastair shook her. 'I'm sorry,' he said. 'Oh, Rosie, I'm sorry.'

They clung to one another.

Alastair said, 'Let's find the key.'

They sank to their knees scrabbling and sweeping at the damp earth. At last her hand clutched something. It wasn't a key. Her fingers explored the object; soft leather, broken stitches through which bulged a woollen-clad foot. A shoe. The figure loomed above her. Rosie gave a gasp and scrabbled backwards until her back struck the bars. The two children clung to one another. The figure moved slowly towards them silhouetted against the flames. She bent down and Rosie saw who it was.

'It's you,' she whispered.

'Yes, it's me, Rosie,' said Grimoulde. She wagged her finger and clicked her tongue. 'Silly Rosie. Took the wrong key, didn't you?'

Rosie nodded.

Grimoulde advanced towards them. She reached into her pocket. Smiling she held up a large brass key. 'This is the one you want.' She turned it slowly. 'And do you know what I'm going to do, Rosie?'

Rosie drew back further. She stammered but couldn't speak.

Grimoulde gripped her by the shoulder. 'I'm going to set you free.' She thrust Rosie to one side. 'D'you hear—free!'

And laughing she placed the key in the lock and turned it.

Rosie and Alastair stared at one another not understanding. Grimoulde pushed open the tiny gate and turned to them. Her laughing face was distorted by the flames and her laughing eyes gleamed orange.

'I'm letting you go, children. I'm giving you your lives back. Shall I tell you why? Shall I?'

Her round face suddenly contorted with fury and loathing. 'Because I hate her. I've always hated her. Always. And now I'm getting my own back, you see. Grimoulde is getting her own back.' She screamed at the top of her voice. 'D'you hear, Sybilla, I'm getting my own back.' She began to laugh once more and pushed them roughly through. 'Go, go,' she shouted. 'Live your lives. Go!'

They scrambled through the door out into the wood.

Sudden sunlight burst upon them and they felt its warmth on their skin and hair. The warm, clear air rang with bird song. Columns of light pierced the shadows. Up in the distance, above the trees where the house lay, a spiral of smoke rose into the air. Red sparks filled the sky.

'The house—it's on fire,' said Rosie.

But Alastair wasn't listening. 'Look,' he whispered. And Rosie turned and gasped with pleasure. Upon a narrow path that descended to a pool stood a small pony cropping the grass.

'Ned!' shouted Alastair.

Ned looked up and Alastair ran forward and flung his arms about the pony's neck. He ran his fingers through his mane.

Rosie looked about her. She hated the forest; hated the way it closed about her like a prison.

'Look,' said Alastair, 'there's the cart.'

'Let's get away from here,' Rosie said.

Grimoulde's laughter had died away.

As quickly as he could Alastair harnessed Ned to the cart once more. 'No reins,' he said. 'Here, Rosie, fetch me that broken piece of strap, that will have to do.'

Deftly he tied the strap to Ned's harness and they both leaped up into the cart. 'Home,' he cried. 'Come on, Ned old boy. Let's go home.'

Ned leaned forward straining to pull the cart up the small slope.

Home, thought Rosie. She smiled at the word.

But there was something wrong. At first she didn't know what it was. Then she knew. She clutched Alastair's arm. 'Listen,' she whispered.

'I can't hear anything,' Alastair said.

'That's what's wrong,' Rosie said. 'The birds. They've stopped singing.' They looked at one another. Alastair clicked his tongue and cracked the whip in the air. 'Come on, Ned. Let's get out of here.'

But even as he spoke a long and terrible scream rent the air. They turned. Rosie's blood ran cold. At the top of the slope standing upright on her black carriage, the reins in her hand, stood Sybilla. Her gown was torn, her face was streaked with dirt and smoke and half her raven hair was scorched away. From the rear of the carriage tongues of flame licked upwards. The scream was now one of triumph. The great stallion wheeled and kicked, his eyes white with terror. Sybilla cracked her whip, lashing it across the stallion's back raising wheals of red. He reared in pain, his hooves danced on air. His head plunged then he crashed to the earth sending the dust and earth flying.

'Look out!' screamed Rosie.

The horse pounded towards them. The earth shook. The whip cracked, and fanned by the wind the flames crackled and roared into the air setting fire to the lower branches of the trees. The cart lay right across the path.

Alastair screamed at the pony. 'Move, Ned. Move!'

But the poor little pony's eyes were filled with abject terror. Fear rooted him to the spot.

'Quick,' screamed Rosie.

Alastair leaped from the carriage pulling off his tunic as he went. The flaming carriage hurtled towards them faster and faster. Alastair flung his jacket over the trembling pony's head. He whispered soothingly and softly in his ear. 'Come, my old dear. Don't let me down now. There's a good fellow. Nothing to be frightened of. Walk, my beauty. Walk.'

Ned's muscles strained. His shoulders heaved and gradually the wheels of the cart rolled forward. Slowly, with Alastair whispering softly in his ear, the old pony pulled the cart up away from the path. Sybilla was upon them. Rosie smelt the acrid stench of burning hair. Felt the pounding horse as he flung past them. Saw the wild eyes of crazed Sybilla as she lashed at her with the whip. The whole carriage was now a roaring fire. Flames licked at Sybilla's gown. She hauled at the reins. Sparks flew from the burning brakes. But it was all too late. In a hiss of flame the carriage, horse, and Sybilla plunged over the abyss and into the dark bottomless pool. The water boiled. Steam rose from its surface.

For a second Rosie and Alastair stared at the place where they had last seen the carriage. Broken branches littered the ground. The water bubbled. And finally was still. A haze of smoke drifted on the air.

Alastair gently backed the cart till they were on the path once more. He pointed Ned up the hill. Neither of them spoke. Alastair clicked his tongue and the horse moved forward. Rosie stared unable to take her eyes from the pool.

'Don't look back,' said Alastair. 'It's dangerous to look back.'

But Rosie couldn't help herself. She had heard a voice singing. Calling. A girl's voice. 'Rosie,' the voice called pitifully from the pool. 'Oh, Rosie.'

She leapt from the moving cart.

'No, Rosie,' shouted Alastair clutching at her. But she brushed away his arm and ran down towards the dark pool. She stood at the very edge staring down into it. How dark and leaden it was.

'Rosie!' It was Alastair calling to her. 'Come back, Rosie, come back.'

She turned to look and as she did so the black waters parted with a rush. She saw for an instant the face of Sybilla, the white and streaming skull, hanks of hair plastered to her face and ears. She heard her scream of triumph before she felt her ankle gripped and felt herself being dragged down the muddy bank. Then she was sinking. Ever downwards until the thick black waters closed over her.

14

Her eyes and mouth filled with water. She kicked out with her leg, struck out with her arms but Sybilla held her like a vice. She could see her eyes, wide staring. The hanks of hair still remaining on her skull streamed upwards swaying like charred seaweed. Bubbles flowed from her half open mouth. And all the time they sank for ever and for ever through the dark water.

She felt her strength ebbing and her will fading. And somehow she didn't care any more. She saw her own hand floating pale before her eyes. My hand, she thought. Mine. And I'm drowning. Rosie's drowning.

Yet somehow she was not afraid. It was as though all this was happening to somebody else; as though she was falling through her own dreams into a never-ending sleep. How good it would be to sleep. Living was such hard work, such an effort. Better to let it all drift away. To let it go. She smiled and closed her eyes. She was at peace. But someone had seized her hair. Was pulling her upwards. Why didn't they leave her alone?

When she forced her tired lids open she saw Aurora's face. Her white dress spread and billowed about her in the waters. She thought of asking about the diary and why she had disappeared that time in the forest. But it didn't seem to matter any more. Nothing mattered.

Silver bubbles streamed through Aurora's hair. Her face was ivory. Her mouth and tongue moved in speech but the words were inside Rosie's head.

'Wake up,' it said. 'Wake up, Rosie. Fight. You must fight and live. Not like me. Fight, Rosie. Live. You must live.'

And then she turned from Rosie and grappled with Sybilla. Rosie watched them twisting and turning in the water. Her ankle was free. She kicked and looking down she watched the two of them sinking downwards, the girl's long hair streaming upwards. Down they dropped turning about each other in a slow and agonizing dance until they were lost to sight in the murky waters.

For me, Rosie thought. She did it for me. But still she felt tired, the weight of the waters seemed to press down on her spirits.

Rosie.

Who was that calling through the rushing water that drummed about her ears? Why didn't they go away? Leave her alone?

Rosie, Rosie, come back to us. Please, Rosie, come back.

And the two voices became louder and louder so that they confused her.

She became angry and struck out with her legs and arms, threshing through the water. *Come back, Rosie.* The voice was like an arm that pulled her upwards. For the first time she felt the pressure on her lungs. She longed for air. Now she had stopped falling and was moving upwards once more. The voices screamed at her. Why didn't they stop?

She forced her way upwards. How much further before she broke through? The water roared in her ears. She could stand it no longer. She opened her mouth and the water flooded in. If only she could scream. Her skull drummed as though it would burst. Still she struck upwards, her strokes ever weaker and more weak. Where was the light? Was it far? And the air? She longed for air. Her body convulsed and heaved. Was there no end to the water?

There was light above her. Light. She reached out for it. Light. Clutched at it. And now the arm had her. It pulled her through into the air, yet still the water tugged at her hungrily. Then the air came into her like a pain. And after the air a light so bright it burned her eyes. And when she opened them once more she saw blinding white discs spinning on a brighter whiteness. So bright that she had to turn her head. And how hard it was to move her head that little way.

Through the water that still filled her eyes she saw the shadow. And the shadow held her. She reached out her hand for the shadow, blinking her eyes. When they cleared she saw it was her father.

'Back,' said her father. 'She's come back.'

And she put out her hand from the sheets which pulled at her like the water. She found his face and his spectacles and the tears that ran down his cheeks and over his chin. And his arm was about her now holding her. And the joy in her was like a flame

102

for she remembered. Knew him to be her father. Knew herself for what she was.

She could hear his voice over and over saying, 'She's come back. Rosie's come back. Nurse, she's come back. Everybody. Everybody. Look, it's Rosie and she's come back.'

Rosie heard the voice and knew he was talking of her.

She really had come back from the dead. The surgeon said it. The sister said it. Her father said it. They came to look at her with kindly curiosity, standing at the bottom of the hospital bed as though she were some strange creature returned from a long and dangerous journey that they could only wonder at.

And this is what she asked her father on the fourth day after her awakening when he came to visit her with a sheaf of papers beneath his arm. She wanted to know how long she had been in the long sleep the doctors called a coma. He kissed her and rubbed her hair and called her his Rip Van Rosie.

'How long? How long?'

'Five days,' he told her. 'Five days and nights.'

And he told her how she had fallen from a broken stairway. And he had thought she was dead. That an ambulance had come and brought her still unconscious to this hospital. And they had wondered perhaps if she might sleep for ever and never wake. That it was a miracle she was alive at all. A miracle.

She thought how strange it was that all this had happened and she had known nothing about it and couldn't remember anything of the accident or the stairway or the five days and nights that followed. When her father asked her what was the last thing she could remember before the long sleep she had to think very hard. But all she could recall was sitting in the car and seeing a lady in a brown coat with a dog in her arms. After that there was nothing.

She felt sad for a moment that something of her life was gone for ever. Was it five days? Had it been really five days she had been asleep? What had happened to those five days? she wondered. She had been there and at the same time not there. It was very strange. Had her father been there all the time, she asked him? Day and night?

103

'The sister was very good to me,' he told her. 'They gave me a bed so that I could be here all the time.'

What had he done while she slept?

'Prayed. Looked at you. Talked.'

Talked? What had he talked about?

'The weather. The book I'm writing.'

'And all that time I was sleeping?'

'Yes.'

It must have been a very one-sided conversation. Didn't he ever run out of things to say?

'Well, a bit,' said her father. He showed her the thick sheaf of papers. 'That's when I started this.'

'What is it?' Rosie asked.

'I started making up a story.'

'About who?'

'About you.'

'Me? A proper book about me?'

'Yes, and your adventures. How you came back from the dead.'

'A real book about me? Can I read it?' begged Rosie. 'I want to read it now.'

'Not yet,' he said. 'When you're a bit better. The sister says you're not to have too much excitement.'

'Is it that exciting?'

'You'll have to wait and see.'

There was something else that worried her.

'Why hasn't Mummy been to see me? Is she all right?'

Her father took her hand. 'Well, I had to tell her a little lie, you see. If I'd told her about the accident and what had happened to you it would have upset her. Especially when the baby was coming. Something might have gone wrong.'

'So what did you say?'

'Oh, I lied.'

Rosie was astonished.

'Daddy! You told a lie! Was it a big one?'

'A whopper. I said you'd gone on a school trip to France. It had come up suddenly and I thought it would be good for you to go.'

'Where did I go?'

'Oh, Paris.'

'Did I have a good time?'

104

'Marvellous.'

'Did Mummy believe you?'

'Of course. I'm a brilliant liar. That's why I can write books.'

'Have you told her now?'

'I told her this morning.'

'What did she do?'

'She hit me.'

'Hard?'

'Quite hard. Then she cried. Then she laughed a bit. Then she cried. And then she laughed again.'

'I'd have liked to see all that crying and laughing.'

Her father smiled. 'Oh, I'm sure she'll do it all again for you if you ask nicely.'

Rosie didn't have to wait long to ask, for just then the doors of the ward were pushed open and her mother entered in a wheelchair. And when she saw Rosie she laughed and cried and laughed just as her father had said. She held a large bundle in her arms. She held up the baby. His feet hung in the air and he goggled at Rosie.

'I want you two to meet each other,' said her mother. She waved the baby's arm. 'This is Rosie. She's called a sister.'

Rosie waved.

'And Rosie, this is your little brother. He's called . . . Well, he hasn't got a name yet.'

She let Rosie hold the baby for a while. His face was red and angry and wrinkled. He waved his little fists at her then yawned very broadly then belched long and loud in Rosie's face.

'That means he likes you,' said her mother.

Rosie held him. 'Hello, little brother,' she said. The baby yawned and fell asleep.

'We'll have to think of a name for him. Any ideas?'

Rosie didn't stop to think. Just said the name. 'Alastair.'

'Alastair?' said her mother. 'Whatever made you think of that? Is it someone you know?'

Rosie thought about it. 'No, I don't think so. It just sort of came out.'

Her mother took the baby from her. She prodded him gently on the chest. 'Do you realize that, my boy? Your name's Alastair.'

The baby slept on.

'He doesn't care,' said Rosie.

'Just like a boy,' said her mother.

Four days later she was packing her things into a suitcase. On the following day she would be going home. She heard the tap of a stick behind her and looking round saw her father. Beside him stood an elderly man with a white moustache and beetling eyebrows.

'You've got a visitor,' said her father. 'Rosie, this is General Westlake.'

The general shook Rosie by the hand. His grip was firm.

'Don't remember me, do you?' he said, his eyes twinkling.

Rosie looked at the lined kindly face.

'I'm sorry, I . . . '

'But I remember you all right,' he said. He sat down, the silver-topped cane between his knees, and smiled. 'You were the young lady who thought my hall was a swimming pool and decided to take a dive.'

'Oh!' Rosie glanced at her father. He was smiling. 'I'm ever so sorry,' she said. 'I can't remember anything.'

'Do you remember coming to the house?'

Rosie sat on the edge of her bed and racked her brain.

Her father interrupted. 'If you'll excuse me, General, I'm just popping up to see Rosie's mother. She's coming out today. Why don't you two have a chat.'

Her father left the ward and the nurse brought the general a cup of tea. He sipped it thoughtfully then smoothed his white moustache.

'I didn't really dive, did I?' said Rosie.

'You must come again one day. I'll show you the dent you made in the flagstones.'

She wasn't sure if he was joking. Then he suddenly winked and smiled. A nurse walked by pushing a trolley. The general nodded after her father. 'Your father's writing a book about me, you know. Biography.'

'Me too,' said Rosie. 'He's writing a book about me.'

'I'm sure yours will be a jolly sight more interesting.' He glanced up at her, then gazed about him then coughed. Rosie thought, Although he's very old and a general he's really quite shy.

'Do you know,' he said suddenly, 'I must be the oldest person in the room. Probably the oldest person in the hospital. Wouldn't be surprised if I wasn't the oldest person in the whole world.' And he laughed. 'Difficult to believe I was ever young, isn't it, eh? But I was, you know. And sometimes it seems like yesterday. The trouble with life is that it happens so fast. One minute it's all there in front of you and the next you've left it all behind.'

'It all seems slow to me,' said Rosie. She wondered if she would ever be as old as the general. It was hard to believe but she supposed it must happen. 'Christmas takes ages coming round,' she said.

'Ah yes,' he sighed, 'I remember the feeling.'

He banged his cane on the floor. 'Oh, and talking of Christmas, that reminds me. I've got a present for you.'

He handed her a small, neatly-wrapped parcel. 'No need to open it now. Keep it for later. I thought it might cheer you up.'

Rosie thanked him. He put down his cup.

'Well,' he said, 'time I was off.'

They shook hands once more. 'I've enjoyed our little chat. Next time your father comes over you must come along with him. Will you do that? If you won't be too bored by an old fogy like me.'

'I'd love to,' Rosie said. 'I can see the flagstones where I dived.'

He laughed and gave a salute and turned to go. Then he turned back. 'By the by,' he said, 'according to your father it's you I've got to thank.'

'Me?' said Rosie.

'Well, he said you chose it.'

She didn't understand. 'Chose what?'

'Why, the name for your baby brother. Alastair. Happens to be my name, you see.' And with a little wave he turned and was gone.

Rosie sat for a moment thinking about the coincidence. Then she sat on the edge of the bed and unwrapped the parcel. It was a book. On the front was a picture of a clown. The title said, *The Book of a Thousand Jokes*. She was beginning to read it when the nurse came in carrying a bundle of clothes.

'We've put them all through the machine,' she said. 'And I put your nail-file, ear-rings and other odds and ends in an envelope.'

Rosie picked up the jeans and the jumper. It was funny thinking that she had been wearing these when she had had the accident. She wondered if she'd left any money in the pockets. It had happened before. In the front pocket was a piece of paper. It might be a five pound note. She drew out a crumpled piece of paper washed white. The faint writing was just about visible. She smoothed out the paper and held it to the light. She could just make out the words.

Edwards, cauli, onions.

She repeated them to herself. Shopping list, she thought. Something itched at the back of her mind. She had a feeling that she'd done this before. Like a dream that you couldn't quite remember when you woke. She shook her head and opened the envelope. She tipped her ear-rings and the nail-file on to the palm of her hand. There was something else; something heavy. She couldn't think what it could be. She tipped it on to the bed; a bronze cross tied to a ribbon. She whispered the words printed on one side. 'For Valour'. She clasped the weight of it in her hand. The medal seemed to burn her palm. For an instant she felt dizzy. Where had it come from? Perhaps the nurse had made a mistake. Mixed somebody else's belongings with hers. Into her mind drifted a vision of a forest, sunlight streaming and a figure in white darting between trees. The dream disappeared as quickly as it had come. There must be a sensible explanation, she thought. There usually was. She would ask her father about it tomorrow. Yes, that's what she would do.

Suddenly she felt immensely sleepy. Since the accident it often happened. She slipped between the sheets, the medal clutched in her hand, and swiftly fell into a deep and dreamless sleep.

And that really was the end of Rosie's adventures. Except for one thing.

A year after the events that you've read about in this book, Rosie went with her father to the town bookshop. The general's biography had been published at last and the two of them were signing copies at a table in the middle of the bookshop. For a time it was fun watching the people buying copies of the book, shaking hands, watching the general and her father signing their names. But after a time she became a little restless. Everybody seemed to ask the same questions and her father and the general seemed to say the same thing each time. She swung her legs and gazed round the shop.

Her father glanced up. 'Getting bored, Rosie?'

'A bit,' said Rosie.

'Why don't you have a look round the Children's Section?'

She didn't really want to look at books. There were hundreds of them at home. 'I'm all right here,' she said.

'Go on. There's something there for you.'

'For me? What is it?'

'I'm not telling you. It's a surprise.'

Rosie wandered down to the section at the back of the book-shop where the children's books were kept. What did he mean? She looked round. A woman was reading a book quietly to her little boy. On a large cushion a girl of about five was looking through a picture book. Rosie turned and suddenly saw her own name on a new display of books. She felt herself going red and looked round to see if anybody had noticed.

The little girl turned over a page.

Rosie wandered over to the display and as casually as she could picked up the book. She read the title. *Rosie No-Name and the Forest of Forgetting*. She read her father's name underneath. She turned a leaf. On the first page was written:

This book is dedicated to Rosie, who came back.

She read her name three times and then turned to the first chapter and began to read. This is what she read:

Just before it all happened Rosie was standing in a country lane watching helplessly as her father drove off the road and into a ditch . . .